A Letter of Truth

Tammy Godfrey

Phoenix Voices Publishing

Contents

Chapter One

My mother's hand was as cold as ice. She looked so pretty in her designer green dress, salon-perfect hair, flawless makeup, and serene expression - one I had never seen...Mom seemed at peace.

Mother had chosen an elegant ebony coffin with gleaming brass fittings. The soft rose pillows set off her dress. Please leave it to my mother to be perfect, even in death, admonishing me for not being like her.

I swallowed and blinked back a fresh stream of tears. I wanted to scream at my mom to get up and stop playing this cruel prank on me. Even seeing her like this, I couldn't accept that such a vibrant woman could have breast cancer. It boggled my mind that she hadn't checked herself.

Setting her hand down gently, I stepped from the casket to stand next to a large wreath of flowers wrapped in cardinal and straw wrap. Those were the colors of the Army, one of the few things we shared. Mom's soldier friends would be out in force at her graveside service but had left the funeral to the family.

I used my drenched tissue to wipe my swollen eyes. Still couldn't... wouldn't start back talking at mom again, even if she wasn't here to snipe back. I'd give anything to have one more chance to argue with her, even if only to hear her express, politely and condescendingly, her profound disappointment that I couldn't be more like her.

God knows I'd tried to be that vibrant, perfect woman like her. But, even though she didn't think of us as anything alike, I knew we shared at least one trait: stubbornness. That's why we were here instead of in California. Her family was from California, but she'd put her foot down in her will, and things would be done her way. The funeral would take place in Sun Valley. At least, I assumed it was because of her will since I wasn't privy to its contents.

The rest of the family had raised hell, but here we were. They hadn't stayed for the whole first day, but they'd be back in force tomorrow for the second viewing day. Then we'd have the funeral on day three and fly back to Pocatello for burial. After that, I'd have to stay yet another day with Oliver since Mother named us both in her will. As her most recent husband, I expected he would walk away with everything she'd treasured, which pissed me off. I couldn't stand him.

The tears flowed again, refusing to obey me. Part of me said crying was okay, but another part warred with that notion. With a sniff, I realized that was pride. It's another trait I shared with my mother, who'd taught me how to make it an art. Pride argued that I couldn't be seen losing control like this in public, even at my mother's funeral viewing. So I had to maintain appearances. I could almost hear my mom whisper in my ear.

I laughed humorlessly through tears. The all-important family pride. Doing what the family expected has worked well for me so far. All that are trying to live up to others' unrealistic expectations had gotten me was two divorces and a distant and sometimes civil - relationship with my parents. Ever since I was a teenager, I'd tried to be just like my mother and be what my father expected me to be. I'd succeeded far beyond my wildest dreams of success. What was that old saying? "Be careful what you wish for because you just might get it."

I'd called my closest friends as soon as I discovered my mother had died. Emma and Charlotte were out of the country with their families. I'd left frantic messages for them, to no avail. Finally, I felt all alone and needed to talk to someone I trusted.

I almost swore at Oliver again. He'd called my assistant yesterday to pass on the news about the funeral. No one had even told me she was ill, much less dead. If Dad hadn't called to coordinate our schedules. But I wouldn't know anything at all. Oliver hadn't mentioned the viewing at all...damn him. When I'd called him back, he insisted that my assistant misunderstood—the lying bastard.

Through the haze of my grief, a cold, arrogant voice said, "If you're going to carry on like this, please take it to the ladies' room." Oliver was back for another go at me. He seemed to screw with me these days. Fine. At least the fury inside me pushed me away from the pain for a little while.

The tears dried up as if by magic, and I could see the bastard standing before me. I could see what attracted my mother to him; he was tall and handsome - the perfect piece of arm candy—knowing my mother, he was fantastic in bed, too. The thought of them together sent a wave of revulsion through me.

"Tell me, Oliver, do you even know why people have viewings for the dead?" I asked.

"Certainly not to carry on like some common piece of trash," he sniffed. "Harper was my wife, and I won't have you disrupting the solemn decorum that she wanted."

I considered taking the massive wreath that Hans and Kat Werner had sent and bashing him with it. I was reaching for it when I yanked myself up short. It'd taken many years and experience for me to think about the consequences before I acted. It still didn't come naturally to me.

I frowned at Oliver's slimy smile. He and I had cordially loathed one another since my mother married him four years ago. Of course, that was partly a lie; we'd never been cordial, but this was out there even for him. Why attack me like this here, of all places?

Movement at the doorway gave me my answer. He wanted to embarrass me in front of someone that mattered. Dad walked in with his wife, Karla. I spared Oliver a glare of pure hatred and schooled my features. I would not disappoint Dad.

"I'll grieve as I see fit. But this isn't over, asshole," I snarled in a low voice.

Sweeping past Oliver as though he weren't there, I went to my father and let him take me into his arms.

His awkward embrace was both comforting in its familiarity and saddening in its brevity. We'd never been more than strangers who just occupied the same house and gene pool. Yet, from the earliest moment I could remember, I knew he was uncomfortable with children, even his own. My father's displays of affection had always been brief and awkward, which never changed in all these years.

I received a perfunctory hug and kiss from Karla, but her eyes didn't reflect the sorrow on her face. I sometimes wondered how a woman like her had taken Dad in. She was only ten years my senior and something of an enhanced Barbie doll.

We were enough alike to disturb me. After marrying two men for their wealth and power, I couldn't very well deride her for doing the same, now could I. The fact that they were still married after almost eight years told me that, at the very least, she was better at handling a romancing husband than I was. Even with her good looks, I knew Dad too well to expect he'd stopped playing the field. I wondered if I would be here in ten years. If I were, would it make him happy?

"I'm so glad to see you both," I said, my voice astonishingly steady. "Thank you for coming."

"Where else would we be, darling?" Dad said in a gruff voice. "You need your family around you at a time like this." But, unfortunately, his glance at his Rolex ruined the effect of those beautiful sentiments.

I almost laughed aloud at such an honest gesture from the man who sired me, whose love I'd worked so hard to get as a teen. But, unfortunately, he was also amazingly like both my ex-husbands. One would think I'd have learned something by watching my mother deal with him, but in the end, I'd ended up marrying men just like him.

I shrugged. Why complain about it? What else was there? All men were alike, weren't they? I had never met or been with anyone who'd make me believe otherwise, though some of my friends seemed happy in their marriages. Emma came to mind. She was genuinely in love with her husband. I didn't like him at first, but he made her happy, so I'd grown to like him over the years.

"Why don't you and Karla go say your goodbyes?" I said with my best hostess face on. "I'm sure you're exhausted from your flight and want to get out to the ranch to rest."

"We should speak to a few people first." With a smile, Dad led Karla to speak with the now solemn and grief-stricken Oliver.

It would be awkward for both men, I hoped.

I felt guilty for being such a bitch. I always was a bitch about something and then felt guilty about it later, though I kept my mouth shut more often than not these days. It was my worst flaw; I'm confident both ex-husbands would agree.

With a sigh, I grabbed my coat, walked out of the funeral home's front door, and looked at the sky. Lead gray clouds hung low above me, promising a good storm tonight. I felt some satisfaction that the weather matched my mood so well.

I shook myself. I'd had enough of this wallowing in self-pity. There'd be time for that once I was away from this place and from Oliver. Part of me longed to return to the ranch; I wanted to reacquaint myself with the bar. Another aspect of me wanted to go back inside and be with my mother. I knew that part of my dark mood resulted from being tired.

After standing there for a little while, I thought I could be in the same room with the rest of them again. The relative lack of viewers told me I hadn't been the only person the self-centered asshole had failed to inform in a timely fashion.

Chapter Two

"Is this Mrs. Masterson's viewing?" A lady asked. I had no idea who she was.

"Yes..." I spoke.

"Sophia, is that you? The last time I saw you, you fit into my arms. You look so much like your father," this woman said.

"Hi, what is your name?" I asked, not wanting to be rude but thinking this would be easier.

"I'm sorry. I'm Kim, your mom and I grew up together. I know a couple of us from the group will be here tomorrow, but I wanted to see her first without them."

"I would like to talk to you later about what my mom was like as a teenager," I said.

"I would love to do that. How about after the funeral before I go back to Pocatello?" Kim said.

"That sounds great," I told her as Kim passed me with a man.

"Sophia, this is my husband, Mike. He also knew your mom. Mike and I were high school sweethearts," Kim said with pride, like being with your high school sweetheart was some tremendous romantic achievement. I don't know. Maybe it was. I gave them a smile. They were so cute together, nothing like I ever saw with my mom and any of her husbands. Kim and Mike loved each other. You could see it in their eyes.

"My mom's husband and dad are inside," I said.

"I've heard everything about them, and all I can say is Phoebe's husband is a piece of work," Kim said. I took a deep breath and just let it out. Have I met her before and forgotten?

Just before I turned back inside, a taxi pulled up, and a ghost from my past, one I'd hoped never to see again, climbed out and paid the cabbie. I wanted to run back inside. I tried to grab the taxi and tell him to head for LA, but I was rooted to the spot. Like a rabbit frozen in fear and unable to run from an advancing snake, I watched him approach with his bag over his shoulder.

"Hey, babe," Daniel said with a grin. "Did you miss me?"

I stood in shock for a moment and then ran back into the funeral home. I slammed the door in his face, holding it closed with my back, trembling. This is going to be the week from hell. This ass hat has been my boyfriend in high school and college; we'd broken up and gotten back together countless times over those years. I'd dumped him for good when I realized that if he were what a boyfriend was "supposed" to be, then it wasn't enough for him. Daniel was total, serially unfaithful, screwing anything with boobs and a pussy. He'd been handsome and rich, a member of my social caste. I'd allowed society's expectations to keep us together or keep getting us back together for far too long. So what in hell was he doing here?

When Daniel knocked on the door, I yelled back as calmly as possible. "Go back into whatever hole you crawled out of!"

"Come on, babe, be reasonable," he pleaded from outside. "I just came to pay my respects to your mother and talk with you. How can that hurt?"

How can that hurt? He had a unique set of memories than I did. Combined with my family's dysfunctions, the entire tumultuous relationship with him had set the tone for every relationship of mine that followed. So while I couldn't blame him for my mistakes, I didn't have to like what he'd done to me.

I was trying to find the lock on the door when Dad, Karla, and Oliver came out, attracted by my yelling.

"Did you say, Daniel, darling?" Dad asked. "Open the door and let him in."

Gritting my teeth, I opened the door and stepped back. Daniel walked in with a smile for everyone. That was his way. He was the golden boy. No one ever believed he did or could do the things he did, and he got off easier than Donald Trump.

Dad smiled and took his hand. "Daniel, my boy! What a pleasant surprise! What brings you from Bermuda on a night like this?" Daniel had fled to Bermuda after beating charges over insider trading, which suited me just fine. Oh, he'd made a show of transferring to Miami to finish his degree. Still, even without proof, I knew the last move to Bermuda was just a continuation of his flight from scrutiny. Daniel worked best under cover of darkness.

"It's good to see you, Mr. Thomas," Daniel said. "I was trying to have a few private words with Sophia to express my condolences and catch up on old times, but I think I've upset her. So I'll go into town, get a room, and leave her some space. I'll see you all after the funeral."

"Oh, I wouldn't hear of it," Oliver said with a malicious smile.

"We have plenty of room, and I insist you stay with us."

My mouth dropped open like a hooked fish. "You've got to be kidding me! There's no way he's staying with me!"

Oliver turned to my father with a raised eyebrow. My father shook his head. "Don't be that way, baby. We have plenty of room, and Daniel is an old friend of the family. He can stay." With a triumphant smile, Oliver walked outside with Daniel.

Daniel shrugged at me, hefted his bag, and followed. Dad hadn't even looked at me. His decision settled the matter. Karla looked at me, though, then she looked at Daniel and smiled. Her desire for Daniel was visible. It was bad enough that I was staying with Dad and his clueless wife and three pit vipers, but now it appeared that one viper had a hunger for another.

"We're calling it a day and going to the ranch," Karla said.

"You're supposed to come with us."

I closed the door, resting my forehead against the excellent wood. Then I started banging my head rhythmically against it. I loved my father, I did, but he made me crazy. "I'm supposed to do a lot of things."

"So, I take it that you and Daniel have a history," Karla continued when I regained control, acting as if I'd never tried to bash my brains out on the door. "But that's over, right?" Her attraction to Daniel turned to lust before my eyes, and for a moment, I considered warning her. Still, I didn't want to share my history with Daniel. Then, with a shrug, I realized they deserved one another.

"It couldn't be more over if he was run over by a bus," I confirmed. "I'm going back for a moment to see Mother again, and then I'll be out." I marched back inside and took a deep breath before walking more calmly to the casket.

After a minute of silence, I went to join my impatient family for the ride to the ranch.

"How about we stop at the Vineyard and go to the wine tasting? This will calm us all down," Oliver stated, and my father agreed. All of them had crammed themselves into Oliver's white SUV. I climbed in next to Dad and sulked to the Vineyard and then to the ranch. This day is getting worse and worse by the minute.

Chapter Three

We all went in and started stripping off our outerwear. Karla looked around the foyer, and I remembered that she'd never been here before. While Mother was alive, she'd never have stood for either Karla or Dad coming here, much less staying here.

It'd been years since I'd been here, and I wanted to refresh my memory of the place, so I gave Karla the tour. The pine entryway opened into a broad stairway that led up to the great room. To either side of the entry were benches. Above them on the walls, hooks waited for coats.

The men stripped off their outerwear and went upstairs. I shrugged off my coat, hung it up, and pulled off my shoes. I motioned for Karla to follow me up to the great room. At one time, I'd thought it was nothing to scream about, but I'd learned to love it and the rest of the place over the years. It had so many beautiful memories. I'd shared it with my parents and with friends. That made me smile. These walls would ruin my reputation, such as it was, if they could talk. Back in college and on selected trips later, my friends and I had had some rough times here before joining the Army. Why the Army? My mom thought I needed to know what I could do, just like her. To be honest, the Army taught me a lot. One of the big things was not to put up with men's bullshit. My mom stood on her own two feet, her rank, and would tell them what they would and would

not do. For me, I was a little more naïve, and it was all about being in love. I loved them. They wouldn't cheat on me.

Wrong!

Karla looked impressed at the vast room, and I felt an unexpected burst of pride. It was over two stories tall, with incredible floor-to-ceiling windows on the far end. The pine paneling that continued from below supported antique ski equipment that added ambiance to the wide-open space. Throughout the room were scattered couches and end tables that fit the spirit of the place like a glove. The stone fireplace took up about half of one wall, and a long, wet bar ran along the opposite side of the room. Two hallways led off, one to the left and one to the right.

I pointed to the glass doors that melded into the large windows. "We have a deck out there with a big hot tub, and there are rooms down each of the hallways. During the screaming match when I arrived, Oliver said, you were in the second room on the left side of the leftmost hall. I'm in the room next to yours." The first room on that side had been my room for as long as I could remember. I'd checked to be sure Oliver was on the opposite side of the house. "There are bathrooms at the end of both halls, and the kitchen is the first door on the right side of the rightmost hall. Now, if you'll excuse me, I need to go change."

When I had my door closed and locked behind me, I threw myself on the bed and held my head. How could things go so badly, so quickly? I hid for half an hour, trying to convince myself it was all a bad dream. Then I gave up, grabbed some clothes, and sequestered myself in the bathroom for a long, hot shower.

The house was quiet when I returned to the great room. Maybe I was alone. A check of the kitchen showed it to be empty and spotless. I walked back out and mixed myself a drink. I needed it. I needed more, but this was all I allowed myself these days.

I'd seated myself on one couch when Daniel came out of my hallway. So much for being alone, I thought. He had changed into a set of slacks and a turtleneck. That was one thing about Daniel. He always cleaned up well. You'd never know about the slime under that slick and handsome exterior.

I took a breath and looked away from him, pretending I was alone. That, of course, didn't work. He fixed himself a drink and sat down across from me.

"I didn't come here to hurt you," he whispered.

My head snapped up. "Forgive me," I said sarcastically, "But I don't see you are coming all this way just to comfort me."

He smiled. "People change. We haven't seen each other in a lot of years. I understand I hurt you, that I disappointed you, and I want to apologize for it. You didn't deserve that."

I blinked in surprise. Daniel apologizing was... unbelievable. I'd have an easier time believing he was gay than he was, sorry. "I... Thank you." The subtle scent of his cologne wormed its way into my senses in unsettling reminders of him.

Against my will, I let him get me talking. The years we'd been a couple worked against me because he knew how to get me to relax my guard. In an hour, the impossible had happened. I was sitting with Daniel and having a civil conversation about what had happened to us in the last two decades. I even listened to his tales of woe about his ex-wives and commiserated with stories about my failed marriages. It was surreal. He refilled my drink when it emptied and was smoother and more polished than I remembered him being. I guessed we'd both matured.

I considered telling him how badly my mother's death had hurt me, but I couldn't imagine being that honest with him. Part of me kept waiting for the other shoe to drop. This had to be a lead-in to something else. Daniel did nothing without reason. Compassion was not one of his failings, and he could never change enough to make it a virtue. I told myself that repeatedly but still felt my will weakening.

Then my alarms went off. How much had I had to drink? I blinked at the smiling Daniel, wary again. He was now sitting on the same couch as I was and had moved uncomfortably close.

Then, looking down, I saw what tripped my alarm. His hand was on my leg. Oh, God! He was making a move on me!

A wave of revulsion mixed with desire flooded through me.

Some of me wanted him, but I would not go there again.

"No," I said, moving his hand from my leg.

Surprisingly, he took that with a nod. "You're right," he said, standing up and returning to the bar. "We might not be ready for that. Still, if I can't help you feel better that way, there are other options." He dug under the bar for a small serving platter and turned his back to me.

"Like what?" I asked, the alarms now screaming inside me. "Daniel, I think I'd better call it a night before we do something that will undo what goodwill we've built up."

"You're right. I have one last peace offering."

He turned around and set the platter on the low table between us, and I suddenly knew where he was going. He'd laid several lines of cocaine on the mirror-bright surface next to an even more enormous pile of the stuff. Part of me wanted to slap it off the table or smash Daniel in the head with it. More frightening, though, another part of me felt the "tingle." Any addict knew about that desire. No matter how long you'd been clean, it never went away. In previous times of stress, I'd felt the draw of that insidious white powder, but I'd managed to avoid slipping. So far.

I watched him pull out the tightly rolled hundred he favored as a "tooter" and snort the lines. Then I gulped when he offered it to me. "No," I said weakly. "I gave that up five years ago. It almost destroyed my life. So I won't go back to it."

"I'm not telling you to start regularly snorting again," he said seductively, "but this is the worst time in your life, and you need something. You just said you didn't have anyone that could be there for you, and you know how a line or two picks you up. You feel good. The pain goes away. Then in a few days, when this is all over, you can just put it back away."

The frightening thing was his logic sounded almost reasonable.

Shaking off the impulse, I dragged myself to my feet. "I should've known this was all an act!" Then I smashed the tray off the table in a cloud of expensive drugs. "You want me to take that, so I'll be back under your control. I remember how it was and what it did to me." I half-turned to stalk off and fired one more shot at Daniel. "I may not toss your sorry ass out of here, but if you value that pretty face, stay away from me."

He grabbed my hand. "Fine, reject me, but I'm doing this for you. This is the only way you'll make it." He slid a small vial into my hand and closed my fingers. "Just in case you change your mind."

I wanted to throw it back in his face, but my instincts and desires warred inside me. Finally, enough of me wanted to do it. I couldn't force myself to throw it away. Instead, I found my hand gripping the vial tightly. "I won't use this," I said defiantly.

In his eyes, I saw a muted flash of something. Was it satisfaction? Then he nodded. "Goodnight, Sophia."

Breathing raggedly, I stumbled into the bathroom. I showered mechanically, scrubbing the feel of the white powder off my arms and then my entire body. When I finally felt clean, I went to my room and locked the door behind me. I set the vial on my dresser and sat on the bed, staring at it. Could I use coke once and then stop again? Would I be ruining my life all over again? Did it matter anymore?

Silkily, the inner voice told me I couldn't hurt any worse than I did now and that Daniel was right. That cocaine would make the pain go away. I could always go back into rehab if I couldn't stop.

I fell back in nervous exhaustion when my hand hit something partially hidden under my pillow. I cautiously opened a small box, hoping it recognized the handwriting immediately. It was from my mom.

Sweetheart

I know if you are reading this that I'm gone. I didn't want you to see me in the final days of my life. I wanted you to remember me as the woman you knew, not what I am right now. There are some secrets I've been hiding from you, and I thought it was time you knew.

As you read, you will discover we are more alike than you thought.

I know you always tried to be like me, but I wanted you to be safe and not do what I did. You will understand what I'm talking about later as you read the letters I left for you. They're all I could find and put up for you. I hope you understand. This was the only way I thought you would understand what I did and why. Remember, I was a teenager, and I didn't fix them. I left them, so you meet the real me at that age.... I think you thought I never loved anyone by my actions, but to be honest, I loved your father so much it hurt. The thing is, I never loved him the way I loved you. I love you so much because you are from both of us...

I hope you will at least find some answers you are looking for in these letters. I'm sorry you found comfort in the drugs, but remember, they won't fix your problems. When you wake from the high or low, the issues will still be there, only much worse. I was going to tell you a long time ago, but you were on drugs then, and I didn't think you could handle knowing the truth then, and I hope learning the truth now doesn't send you back to drugs. I saw things in you that your father had done which scared me to death. So please don't judge me for what I have done. I was trying to protect you. Love Mom

I looked into the shoe box and thought I could read them tomorrow after the viewing. I put the box under my bed, stripped off my robe, and turned off the lights, but I could still feel the siren call of the white powder in the darkness. I then turned back on the lights and grabbed the box. I pulled the lid off and took out the first letter. They were numbered.

May 1

Damian,

Hey, babe, whatcha doing? Not much here. Just thinking about how you feel sorry about Curtis, I know how much he meant to you out of all people. I also know what it's like to lose someone close to you to such a horrible thing. It makes you wonder, ya know? I'm glad you guys decided to be friends, so it wouldn't hurt you as bad, ya know.

I'm so glad you asked me out while he was still alive, though I don't feel it's behind his back or anything. You know it is disrespectful to his grave. I love you so much, baby. I hate to see you like this. Think of how much pain is actually gone now. Now you can miss him instead of hating and loving him. All at the same time... like a brilliant man once told me, "Love is something you get when you die."

Well, call me later, okay?

Love you always and forever, Phoebe

P/S I love you.

Cheer up, Charlie.

Jill loved the threesome.

She said it was fun, but it hurt at first.

Threesome? Really mom? I folded the letter or note because they were notes from when she was from school, but still, I grabbed letter two and started reading

May 13, 1999

Damian,

Hey, sexy, what are you up to? Not a lot here. Just sitting here thinking about your fine ass, as usual. Anyway, sorry I didn't make it over there. I fell asleep somewhere around eleven. I'll talk to Curtis today and see what he says, okay? How are you feeling today? Are your shoulders better? How are you gonna fuck me if your shoulders are killing ya? Just wondering.

What a beautiful day, huh? I can't wait until this weekend. I'm gonna miss you. I wish you could go with me. I love it up there. It's so fuckin cool. You're gonna love it too. I want to fuck you in the water. But, damn baby, now makes that sound?

Well, I better go. I'm not gonna worry about telling you to write back because I already know I can fuck that. I will see you later,

Loving you always,

Phoebe

Why am I reading these letters? I knew if I dithered long enough in making my decision, I'd probably give in, and the voice seized on that to urge me not to fight anymore. So I put the letter away and knew I would read more tomorrow. So I was still wrestling with my demons when I fell asleep. I couldn't help but wonder, not about Daniel's misguided motivations, not about my addiction. I couldn't help but wonder where the box on my bed came from? Who put it there?

Chapter Four

It was pitch black outside when I woke up needing to use the restroom. The clock on the nightstand said it was a little before six in the morning. My mouth tasted terrible. That wouldn't do. I had to take a toothbrush to my teeth right now.

I grabbed a robe and wrapped it around myself. It was too early for this crowd to be up, but there was no way I was taking chances around Daniel. I hurried out of my room toward the bathroom and stopped dead. Five feet away, staring at me with equal surprise, was Karla.

She didn't let that surprise stop her from closing Daniel's door behind her and holding a finger up to her lips. Her robe was loose; her hair was in wild disarray. Even after all that bastard had done, and all the time passed, I still felt a momentary surge of jealousy. With a snort to myself, I forced it down. I was an idiot to have any emotion for Daniel other than contempt.

I smiled and shook my head. Dad had outdone himself in getting a woman that suited him this time. I wondered if he knew his sweetie was sleeping around on him. If he knew, did he care? Regardless, I didn't. I motioned for her to go on without saying a word. Neither Daniel's past nor Karla's present infidelity was my problem. Dad didn't know that someone was diddling his darling on the side. It only sounded like fitting justice to me.

Karla opened Dad's door with a languid smile and slipped back inside.

I locked the bathroom door behind me since I didn't want Daniel walking in on me. Daniel had a bad habit of doing that to my friends and me. So I did my business and showered so I could dress and get the hell out of this cursed place before people started getting up. The last day of the viewing would be soon enough to look at them.

As I dressed in my room a few minutes later, I kept glancing at the vial of cocaine. My hand itched to put it in my purse, just in case. I almost did, but in the end, I grabbed the following three notes, leaving the cocaine where it was, and I left it there and locked my door behind me on the way out. After that, I did not need to worry someone might see it. The maid would leave the locked room alone in her morning cleaning rounds.

I smiled as I boosted Oliver's spare keys from the hook by the door and let myself out. Of course, I could take one of the other cars in the three-car garage, but this would piss him off, making it the perfect choice.

In a few minutes, I had his SUV on the road into town, and my stomach was growling. I tried to find a place that was open for breakfast this early. And it needed to be somewhere I wouldn't run into any of Mother's family.

The first place I saw that fit the bill was one of those all-night diners. It looked like it should have had a flickering neon sign. The coffee was going to rip the lining out of my stomach. Screw it. I parked and walked in past two truckers on their way out. I saw them stare at me and knew I didn't quite fit the usual mold in this place. Good.

The waitress that seated me looked a little worse for wear. Her frazzled bottle-red hair threatened to escape from her hairnet in the same way her tits tried to escape her low-cut top.

But, in this crowd, that earned some excellent tips.

"What'll it be, Hon?" She sounded like she should give up her two-pack-a-day habit while she still had a throat. I looked at the menu. "What won't kill me?"

The waitress - Alice, her tag read - laughed. "If I had a nickel for every time I heard that. Go with the omelets, and the coffee isn't too bad."

"Fine," I said. "Give me a veggie omelet, no onions, and a coffee."

"You got it."

I couldn't help but wonder if the sway in hips was for my benefit or just out of habit. Either way. I forgot about her as soon as she swayed off to another table. I let the black cloud of thoughts flow over me and put my head into my hands. This depression and anger always seemed to wait for a chance to slip into my head. My life sucked.

I shook my head to force the negative thoughts out. Fighting these black moods and self-criticism was a never-ending battle. I knew I wasn't fair to myself. Until Mother died, I'd had my life turned around, at least some. Emma and Charlotte had turned my life around.

Emma, especially, had told me I needed to change. She'd been pretty firm, too. I yelled and screamed. I threw a tantrum.

I sulked. When the choice became clear that I'd lose my best friends if I didn't do something, I started changing. Years later,

with what seemed like their tireless support, I was still fighting to change., I'd discovered I didn't know who Sophia Thomas was, though I'd started looking forward to meeting her in the last few years.

After a few minutes, when Alice set the coffee on the table, I dragged myself back from the depths of my thoughts. I looked into the parking lot while sipping the paint thinner she called 'not too bad' coffee. I think I was wrong. She didn't smoke at all. She just drank this stuff.

I looked in my purse, took the notes, and opened the first letter. It was a long letter with a sticky note in my mom's handwriting.

Sweetie

He was stoned when he wrote it, but I learned more about Damian's feelings than when he was sober.

Mom

June 24,1999

Phoebe,

Hi! How are you feeling, Little Bean? Anyhow, how ya doing?

Me: Okay- just being bored waiting for your lunch and after school.

I'm excited! How has your day at school been? So far, good, ah? But, of course, the rest of the day will be the shit too. How do you feel? High yeah, my mission wasn't impossible! I'm weird. I know.

Ya, spoiled little brat! I thought I spoiled Curtis, but you will be next! Geez... don't get addicted. I know what it's like, whether you are or not. So don't fuck with me. I promise I will never give it to you. Just have to stay sober, ah? That would be better. Today, the last time I do it with Lance, he's scaring me. I told Joe, and he thinks I'm stupid because he's only sixteen and could get addicted, and I would kill myself if he did. I'd feel guilty! Too damn guilty. I don't know what I'd do. I've watched too many fucking friends get hooked on the shit, and it sucks to watch, especially when I have seen Curtis.

I about died.

You can only help yourself, and I didn't know what to do. Nobody can help you. So, I didn't know how to handle it or help him. Time. That's all that counts. I never want to go through that much hurt again, not with someone.

So close to me. Not again. I would die this time. I don't know if I should smoke any with Curtis. It would be too hard for me to go through that again.... I hope to God you two don't! I would fucken go crazy and kill myself! Just trust me, babe. I've had plenty of experience! Never again will it happen. I will talk to Curtis too, and if I decide to take that chance, it doesn't happen again. But, please, I beg you to remember if you do. I will always be here, and nobody can help you. Only you can help yourself! Take it from me,

God! I hope it doesn't happen to Curtis again. I swear I'd fucken kill myself

from so much guilt and madness I'd go crazy!! Shit...

I watched Katie and Jamie get hooked; it wasn't a pleasant sight! It hurt Joe and me, and we took the blame because we got them started. You should have seen them, Phoebe. I didn't know them anymore. I didn't even know myself. It's just sick! I'm scared! I mean for Curtis and you and Lance and Jill. You can only help yourself. Damn, this is pretty serious shit. I'm getting everybody started again. GOD, I hope it doesn't take my Curtis!!! I fucken hope to God! Fuck see, listen to me.

I'm already tripping, and it's only nine in the morning, and it won't happen till after school. Should I or shouldn't I invite Curtis to try meth? Could you give me advice, Phoebe? I don't know what to do... I'm so confused now. Please tell me I'm doing the right thing by not asking him. Or tell me I'm right. I don't know, though. I'd also feel pretty bad if Amber turns into a big rock head too! It was only her first time, and she could get hooked! Honesty, Lance wants to buy it for his first or second time. My parents would disown me and kick me out for not being a big brother he looked up to and admired. Plus, the church they belong to will have a fit. They would kill me for turning their baby into a meth head. They'd turn to me if they found out before anyone else. My mom did with Thalia. I don't give it to her anymore because my mom caught her or us. She was crying and telling Thalia to think twice. All was my fault, and I'm worthless. Their parents are trying to save Thalia and Lance before it's too late. It was too late, and I couldn't help; I was just encouraged. I felt pretty bad. That's why I stopped too. Now look, I'm there again. Shit, I am worthless.

I could have been better and wouldn't be a faggot if I'd just listened to my brother when he talked to me. He thought I was on it, but I'd never tried the shit before. He was crying to me, saying I was fucked up. I felt so bad because I wasn't even in it. After that, I promised myself I'd never do it because it would hurt my family and me. Well, I started, and it hurt everybody now. Look at me now; I'm so lazy. I'm fucken addicted and worthless now. I don't go to school; I don't have a job. I'm fucken living off my parents. What a life, huh? Do you want that? Well, it will happen. You don't think, but someday you get caught up in all the fucken shit.

I was killed. I admit it, and I'm fucken worthless and low-life. I found out there's no point, but there is somewhere. It's just drugs that led me to believe there isn't.... it sucks. I'm telling you to remember I've had experience, and you're just watching if you don't watch yourself, girl. It'll catch up to you eventually!! Promise. So chill out after this. If I didn't, I'd let you turn into an addictive no good, low-life scum. But I care, and you can do better if I know you. Just promise me please.... okay. Say, I promise Damian right now...

Thanks!! I'm just terrified now! What should I do about Curtis now, though? I already talked to Lance this morning when we were doing it. It was sad. He almost cried. I guess he didn't know I'd care that much for him. Well, he's got another thing coming! I already talked to Thalia a long time ago when she and I were doing it. I think she got the point, though. I wouldn't give it to her anymore after that time, so don't ask, but she still does something, but I say No! Sorry, I can't do that to your Dad and my mom again and everybody who cares. So now I'm stuck in this position once again. Oh, dear. What am I to do? I guess there's nothing else because I sure in the hell aren't going to sit here and watch my family and my life tumble to the ground again.

I started picking myself back up again from losing Curtis and watching him walk out of my life. I couldn't even stop him when I knew I could have if I had never opened my big mouth to everybody like a dumb ass!

I would still be so happy and have everything I've always dreamed of having and just being so kind and cheerful. I wish!

Never again can I put up with that shit in love, and I wouldn't hurt you. I'd be hurting myself all over again. Life would suck once again. Who cares! I used to say to myself. I didn't care about anything or no one. Why should I if I'm the only one? If I want to care about the only one, why should I walk out of my life without a sign or a word, just being a dick and hurting me more? Life Sucks Once Again! I just let everybody down again. I just let everybody down again! I regret telling you or anybody about Curtis and me, but like I said, what was I to do? I would be dead now if I hadn't ever spoken to anyone. Try about eight months ago. My soul would be old, and never again will I be told. OLD News. He's dead. Move on with this miserable life. That's what I think if I had never told you or if Joe had never found out. When Joe didn't know, Curtis hit me and choked me for no reason. Oh, because I was lying beside my boyfriend, he had a little tizzy fit and started doing that shit.

I got sick of it, and I was going to stab myself with a knife. I was going to stab Curtis if he touched me again. I was so sick of it! I couldn't handle his abuse and bullshit. Then when I was about to stab myself, I was like, Curtis, I'm going to stab myself if you touch me once more. He felt me once more like a dick, and I said, Okay, here I go, and I was ready, but he tried to take the knife away, and it cut up my hands. Curtis thought I stabbed myself, so he jumped up, turned the light on, and was freaking out. So, Joe woke up, wondered why Curtis stabbed me, and told us to get out. Both were mad at each other, but Curtis went home, and I went back downstairs and went back to bed. The next day, Joe asked me what the fuck was going on last night. I told him everything because I was tired of being abused or hurt every night. Curtis told me to spend the night with him at Joe's house. He heard us having sex plenty of times and Curtis making me give him a fucken blow job at my best friend's house, who is disgusted at the shit. Both Curtis and I know he is fucken listening to us. You know how gross that is.

To find out your best friend is gay and screwing and getting cum stains all over the fucken bed. Do you know how that made me feel? Like shit, Joe and I have been friends for a long time, and he knew me better than that. We've been going to school with each other since kindergarten. We've been good friends since we moved here. I felt embarrassed and humiliated, and disgusted by it too. Joe got over it but knows all he does is tease me because I couldn't say no or wait for Curtis. That is how Joe found out. It's just that Curtis would always tell me to spend the night with him at Joe's, and the same shit happened every fucking weekend. Joe would hear us, too. Every time, every fucken time, that is so fucken gross.

Curtis says it's my fault, but he forced me to suck his dick and fuck me up the ass. I couldn't blame Joe for feeling the way he does and feeling so disgusted, especially while trying to sleep. Shit, that's fucken gross. Curtis believes it's all my fault. Everyone knows, of course, there's nothing to change his fucken mind. Whatever he says goes. Fucken stupid. I didn't care what anybody thought because I loved Curtis so damn much. I didn't want to manage or hear what anybody had to say about us. He did, though he cared a lot about what people said or did, I guess. He was embarrassed or something, embarrassed by me.

Then he says he loves me. Yeah, right. That's supposed to make me think he does if he can't show or tell me off or be proud of me, you know. I couldn't handle it. I said nothing because I didn't want to lose him, but I put my fucken foot down. It would be my way too, or at least what I thought from then on cause Curtis wasn't my Dad. He sure in the hell wasn't going to tell me what to do anymore! I was fed up with it. No more for me. That's when he started being a dick face and a jerk. It seems like his way or no way.

Fuck that shit. That's bullshit! Right? You don't know; the real side of Curtis is cruel and selfish and a crybaby too. Everybody has another side to them, but you've already seen mine. You just haven't seen Curtis's other side. Oh well. Shit, he makes me so mad. Then I loved him so much as if he was my Dad. I don't know, although I just fucked up. I'm sick of all of it, though. I've never experienced so much Goddamn pain, love, and happiness in my whole life. He was fucken running me out of life. So fast a fucken good too. He almost killed me. It sucked. I never want to be like that again. Manic depression. It almost killed me. I was sick for a while too. Remember when I was puking. I wouldn't say I liked it later. I was blood, yuk.

It was gross, but I sound stupid now, huh?

I'm just fucken weird, that's all. I think I've lost it.

I'm just sick of all this shit, and the only things that make me happy are Meth, Jill, and you. I'm grateful. Thanks. I appreciate it. Never will I forget you two; I hope we all three never part. So, we must move together and live together no matter what relationship or friendship. You three will always be together forever. Promise you're the only one who understands and sticks with me through thick and thin, and I am grateful. I love you and have you for good.

Phoebe, you and I have to promise right now. We will never part from each other for as long as we live, no matter what.

Always and forever.

Well, Baby, I will stop writing and give it to Katie, and Jamie's coming over. See you at the party tonight.

Love ya, Damian

Chapter Five

Why is she having me read a letter from this person, Damian? I looked out the window to see a beatenup, muddy Land Rover lumbering into the parking lot. A man in a worn leather bomber jacket climbed out and stretched. My impression placed him as a construction worker. A handsome construction worker, he looked a lot better than the average customer in this joint did. Forget this joint. He looked a lot better than most men anywhere did. Fit and trim, he probably worked out.

He walked up to the doorway and smiled at Alice while she flirted with him. I gave him an automatic once-over as she led him toward the empty table next to mine. Tall, with a ruggedly handsome face and dark eyes framed in the straight black hat that fell to his shoulders. It was hard to be confident with the beat-up leather jacket covering his torso, but he seemed muscular. His walk exuded an air of confidence without the usual arrogance. That was an unusual combination in men, in my experience.

When he stopped beside my table, I knew what was coming next: the come on. Men only had one thing on their minds.

His words startled me, though. "You're Sophia Thomas, right?" "Do I know you?" I asked with a frown.

His lips curved a little. "Probably not, but I know you. I'm Anthony Ricco. I'm so sorry to hear about your mother." He

offered me his hand, and I shook it automatically while trying to recall the name.

When I placed it, my frown deepened? "I remember someone by that name, but he was my father's age," I said. "A big guy, kind of, you know, round."

He nodded. "That's my Dad, Big Tony. I came with him to see your Dad a few times when we were teenagers. The round part happens to men in my family if they don't work out," he added with a grin, "and even my father would tell you that since he never works out, he's fatter than hell. Mind if I join you?"

My memory clicked. I remembered him, a skinny kid who resented his father dragging him around. I remember overhearing his father tell Dad he thought his kid would give him a stroke, end up in prison, or, more likely, both. After hearing Dad agree with his friend, I avoided the kid.

Well, that was then, and this was now. So, I wasn't inclined to let Dad take my calls anymore.

"Sure, have a seat. I remember you now," I said with a nod. "So, if your dad is Big Tony, does that make you Little Tony?"

He shrugged as he sat, although I saw the barest flicker - an echo of some long-ago pain - in his eyes. "I go by Tony. I don't like being compared to my father." He looked at Alice and pointed at me. "I'll take whatever she's having."

"Okay, Tony, it is," I said as Alice sashayed back. "I didn't think you knew my mother or father so well."

"I don't," he agreed. "My Dad got the word too late to make it here. I'm here for work, so Dad called to ask me to come to his place. So, you know, wave the family flag."

That I understood all too well, "Mine usually just tells me he wants me somewhere and then expects me to obey."

Tony laughed. "My father lost that hold on me when he disowned me and tossed my sorry ass out of his house on my seventeenth birthday."

I sucked in my breath. "He disowned you. That's terrible! If he did that, why come here for him at all?"

Tony shrugged again. "I'm not here for him. I'm here for myself. I'm a Di Ricco, and we pay our debts in money and honor. My family should be here for yours, so I'm here." I nodded, impressed despite myself.

"Besides, throwing me out was the right thing to do," he continued, "even if I didn't like it. I was a real punk. In his place, I'd have thrown myself out, too."

"Wow." I knew that Dad, Karla, and Oliver understood money. Still, I doubted any of them even knew that honor existed. I shook my head and leaned back as my omelet arrived. Alice smiled at Tony. "I put a rush on yours, sugar." I took a bite and decided it wasn't immediately fatal.

Tony smiled at Alice. "Thanks." Then he stood and took off his jacket; I was right about him working out. His black tee shirt did nothing to hide his solid physique.

I felt a moment of physical longing but repressed it. The last thing I needed was a complication like him in my life. Other women could have casual flings, but I'd never been able to be that way. If I slept with a man, it was because we were in a relationship for the long haul - not that the long haul ever seemed to last over three or four years for me. But men being men, I doubted that my four-year record was in danger.

"What do you do for a living?" I asked as I continued to pick.

"I'm in construction," he said, confirming my first impression. "We're building an apartment complex at a job site about a hundred miles down the highway."

I'd guessed right. I smiled. Too bad a relationship was out of the question. Still, it was for the best. He'd use me for my body and money and then cheat on me despite both. He was a man, after all.

"That sounds very interesting," I said politely.

"No, it doesn't," he replied with a grin. "I can tell that swinging a hammer isn't very interesting to you, but that's okay," he said, forestalling my objection as his expression sobered. "If there's anything that I can do for you, all you have to do is ask. I didn't know your mother, but I realized she loved you. I could see it even when I was a kid."

Men rarely surprised me, not even when I found out they'd been sleeping around. "If I need to ask you for something, how would I get hold of you?" I finally got out. I figured it was time for the line about how if I wanted to get a hold of him, all I had to do was put my hand out.

Instead, he dug out a worn leather wallet and pulled out a card. He flipped it over to write on it. "Here's my cell number," he said. "If you need anything at all, call me. day or night." He handed me the card, and I looked at the numbers written in a firm hand. A flip of the card showed it wasn't his card. Instead, it was for some truck stop. I could only imagine why a man would have the number for a truck stop in his wallet. I'll never understand men.

I slid the card into my purse and considered him silently as his plate arrived, and he seasoned it to taste. "Do you miss the world you had when you were growing up?" I asked.

He grinned at me and took another bite of his omelet. "What's not to miss? Having money to burn is great, plus having my Dad try to mold me into someone just like him? But frankly, I'm better off not having everything laid out for me." he waved his fork at me. "Not that I'm better than anyone else."

There was some pride in there. He and I had a lot in common.

A lot more than met the eye, I thought.

"So, you were a rebel without a clue?" I asked. "Trying to find a place and a way for yourself?"

"Oh, hell no! I knew what my goal in life was; I was a pain in my father's ass," he said. "People think it's easier to be rich. We both know that's not true. Hell, if I'd gotten a tattoo back then, my Dad would have tossed me out even faster."

"You have a tattoo?" I asked with more interest than I'd expected and more than I'd intended to let on. I'd considered getting one when I was younger, but the horror stories were too much to get past. "What kind?"

"A mermaid - on my left butt-cheek," he said before taking a sip of his coffee.

"Bull," I said with an unladylike snort. "No way do you have a mermaid on your ass."

"True enough. The tattoo is classified, so I must spread false stories to keep my adoring public guessing."

I shook my head and smiled at him. "I bet. Do you keep a club in the car to drive them back?"

"It's a Louisville Slugger. Works every time."

We ate and talked about our lives as spoiled rich kids for almost an hour, though it seemed only a few minutes. When I looked at my watch, I thought we had plenty of time to keep talking, and I was shocked to see that the funeral home would open in less than twenty minutes. The quick burn of disappointment surprised me, both in its depth and because I'd felt it at all.

I didn't know when I'd been so comfortable sitting and talking with a man. I supposed our shared past helped, but he was neither fish nor fowl. Tony wasn't a rich guy who grew up like Daniel or a poor schmuck like the truckers who shared the diner and an outspoken fondness for large breasts. He differed from the men I'd associated with in the past. Tony was exotic.

Part of me wanted to stay right here talking with him. That made me feel closer to him than I'd ever felt to anyone outside my clique. I'd never been chatty with guys, but I felt a connection with Tony that I'd never expected.

Regretfully, I grabbed my purse. "I've got to go to the funeral home. I wish we had more time to talk because it's been fun."

He pulled out a twenty and tossed it on the table, silencing my objections. "If I can't spend my money on breakfast with a friend, why have it? I'm going to go to the viewing and be here for the funeral, too, so we can talk again."

"I'd like that."

His hand briefly touched mine as he stood up. An electric tingle unsettled my stomach. I reminded myself that I didn't need this kind of entanglement, that he was just a man and couldn't be trusted, even if part of me seemed to want to trust him. Even with everything Emma and Charlotte had done to help me, I still couldn't trust men. I could almost feel Emma frowning at me and sighing.

"Let's set something up before we leave the viewing, then," I said, deciding to go with my emotions rather than my brain.

He smiled as he slid his jacket on. "I'd like that. I'll see you there." I watched Tony's perfect ass walk out the door and sighed. I headed for the ladies' room. God willing, I wouldn't catch anything in there.

Chapter Six

When I arrived at the funeral home, Tony was talking with Dad. I could tell Dad did not know who he was and that he was getting an abbreviated form of the same I'd gotten. Karla was giving Tony the eye from behind Dad. I recognized the look. While her behavior didn't surprise me, the sudden spike of jealousy stunned me.

What the hell was that? I'd just met the guy, and already I wanted to club the competition in the head like a baby seal? Was I seeing her as a competition? That surprised me even more. But, of course, he wasn't mine, and I wasn't dating him, so that thought had no place in my head. I forced it back down, composed my features, and walked up to them.

"There's no need to stay in a hotel. We have plenty of room at the ranch," Dad said.

Tony shook his head. "That's unnecessary, sir. I don't want to disturb your family."

"You won't be," Karla said with a wide smile. "We wouldn't hear of it. So you're staying with us, and that's final."

That last bit was loud enough for Oliver to overhear from his post beside the coffin. He hurried up, smoothing a sudden worried look. "Hello, I'm Oliver. What's this about the ranch?"

"I've decided that Tony should stay with us tonight rather than at a motel," Dad said with a smile. "It makes no sense to see all that space go to waste."

Oliver was looking for a way to back out of that commitment from his facial expression before it became final. I was sorry about Tony being trapped with Karla, but I wasn't about to let Oliver have his way.

"Dad's right," I agreed, stepping up beside my father. "We have six rooms, and the place would rattle with all of us alone. So please, Tony, take a spare room. It's no trouble."

Karla shot me a calculating look. Then she nodded, her brain already working the angles. "Yes, Tony. Please do," Karla added.

So, we're we a fine pair of conniving bitches?

Trapped, Oliver nodded. "Of course, we'd be happy to have you."

"Well, since you all insist, I'll do it," Tony said, glancing at Karla. Right then, I knew that whatever else he might be, he was more intelligent than the average bear.

That thought was so arrogant that I snorted at myself. That got me a frown from everyone. I coughed to cover my slip-up.

"Sorry, my throat's dry."

Dad quirked an eyebrow at me and headed for the front door with Karla on his arm. Oliver seized the moment to cut Tony off and start talking. Oliver loved to speak, and his favorite subject was himself. I sat close to my mom, pulled out one note my mom had given me, and opened it. It looked like a note on old computer paper from when they still had the paper with holes on the side. I smiled, remembering mom telling me she had to write programs for computer class, so this had to be one.

Damian,

Please read this even though you don't want to, and you don't after I caught you last night with Curtis at the party and that long letter you wrote me about Curtis. You were fucking him when I found you and the yelling you did afterward. So now it's my turn to talk.

I'm sorry you didn't want to be friends. That's a shame since we know more about each other than anybody knows about us. I want you to know that I still won't tell anybody, and I expect the same respect from you, even though you believe I don't deserve any. I am a hypocrite, and while I thought you felt I didn't deserve any, so are you. I am a hypocrite, but I thought of another way too. We both tried to commit suicide, and one told the other not to. Why did you pretend to care? Why didn't you just let me do it to get me out of your short hair? I WOULD DO IT when I got back into my room, but you were waiting for me, not understanding shit. Well, fuck it. I don't want to understand. I don't want you anymore, Damian, and I hope you're happy. You'll always have a special place in my memory that's unique to anyone else, but I can move on with my life. Thanks for everything, but I'm not a liar, stealer or snitch. Okay, so remember that, alright? There are only two things I've ever asked you to recognize, and that's one. You should know the other one.

Remember always.

I have one last question. If you knew you were in love with someone already, why did you even start a relationship with anyone else? That's not fair to anybody. Think about it.

Well, I'm sorry it had to end like this, Damian. Maybe someday we can be friends. Until then, have an excellent life,

Love always,

Phoebe

P/S I wish Curtis and you a happy life together.

As I looked on, dozens of my mother's family were milling around her casket. I tucked the letter back into my purse, not knowing why she wanted me to read it or if any of them weren't helping; they were confusing. I stood, slipped to the side of the room, and returned to the area near Mother. I folded the note and put it back in my purse. Two older women were looking at her and speaking in low tones to one another. Not low enough for me to miss hearing.

"It's a terrible shame, her having a daughter like that," one of them said. She was some great aunt. The woman next to her was her sister. The matching sour expressions were a good clue about that. Her words solidified my anger and gave it focus.

"Yes," her sister agreed. "Sophia had such potential and was such a great disappointment to her mother. She married well enough, but her other habits," she tisked.

I wondered which of my failings she meant. God knows I'd had enough of them to piss my mother off.

"I mean! She's one of those drug-sniffing hippies," my greataunt said.

I almost laughed. She thought I was a hippie. Puh-leeze! I've seen all the pictures of my great aunt and her sixties lifestyle. I returned from Iraq and couldn't handle what I saw and did. Most of my friends at the time were using weed and then cocaine, which was so easy to get.

"All those rumors about her and..." she looked around and lowered her voice. A spike of pain shot through my head as my heartbeat thundered in my ears. The room turned red. I shoved the wreath to the side, and it fell with a crash. The sisters recoiled from me as if I were the devil herself.

"She was never ashamed of me!" I snarled. "You don't know me! You don't know a thing about my relationship with my mother! How dare you?"

Oliver was there in a flash. "That is enough! You've disgraced yourself and our family," he boasted. "Get out."

"You," I said, turning on him, "are full of it, too. Do you think marrying into a family makes it yours? You're even more of an outsider than I am, you poser. My mother may have married you, but she at least loved me."

He waggled a finger in my face and glared. "Go call one of your little dyke friends for a drug party and leave the people that loved your mother alone to grieve! But, of course, you're drugged out, or you wouldn't behave like this in front of your mother."

No one talked about my friends that way. No one!

I leaped at him.

Someone snatched me out of the air. I kicked and screamed at Oliver while my abductor carried me toward the front door over his shoulder. Like a sack of potatoes.

"Let me go! Let! Me! Go!" I said, beating on the leather-clad back. It was Tony. Why was he taking me out of here like this when I needed to shred that bastard Oliver?

He grabbed my coat off the hook and carried me into the parking lot. "I don't think so," he said, setting me down beside Oliver's SUV. I went around him and went back inside, but he blocked me. "That's what he wants," he said. "Can't you see that? He's baiting you."

"So what? I'll give him what he wants, and you call the paramedics."

"Save it," he said, planting an arm in front of me again. "Save it for later when they won't find the body."

I turned my head at the comment. The innocent grin I saw on his face broke my fury, and I took a deep breath and forced myself to turn away from him. I put my clenched fists on the hood in front of me. The visual of Oliver beating to a bloody pulp helped calm me enough and turned my snarl into a brief smile. Unfortunately, my head was pounding, and I lost that smile as I realized Tony was right. I'd fallen right into Oliver's trap. He wanted to portray me in the worst light possible in front of many people. I'd stepped right up to the plate when those women started gossiping. What did I care what they thought, anyway? Dammit!

I nodded. "You're right. As much as I hate it," I grated out. My hands twitched with adrenaline withdrawal. "I thought I'd changed, but underneath I can still see the college girl in me. I'm sorry. I shouldn't act without thinking because it's what my emotions tell me to do."

"You don't need to apologize to me. We need to leave, but we can come back later when most people have left," he said. His voice was calm, and it didn't sound like an order. It just sounded reasonable. That was strange. Only those who knew me best could talk me down like this when I was tearful. My mind shied away from how he could do that.

"I'd rather go back in there and cut off his balls," I muttered. "If I could find them."

"There's always time for that later," he said again, touching my shoulder. Then, I realized that the cold was seeping through without my coat on and his hand felt warm, almost hot, against me. That sent the last anger running away, and a jolt of need replaced it, a condition I couldn't allow myself to act on. So instead, I picked up my coat from where he'd set it down and slid into it.

I stepped to the driver's door, pulling away without appearing too apprehensive. It was slight. "I need to go somewhere, but

where should we go? What should we do?"

"Do you know how to ice skate?"

I stared at him over the hood in disbelief. "Ice-skate at a time like this?"

He grinned. "Trust me."

With a sigh, I gave in and climbed into the SUV. So, he wanted to go ice-skating. What other surprises would this man spring on me next?

Chapter Seven

I laughed at how impulsive and out of character this was, even for me. Then, finally, Tony looked up from tying on his skates and grinned. "What?"

"This," I said, waving my hand at the small crowd of kids and adults filling the rink. "What the hell am I doing here?"

My subconscious supplied its answer. My two ex-husbands had been right about one thing regarding me; I was a hedonist. Even though it hurt others, I had a weakness for doing something that pleased me. I liked to luxuriate in pleasure and comfort.

Sex had always been a part of that. So was the cocaine. Perhaps especially the cocaine, it made me forget. Hard knocks had shown me I had to have limits in seeking my pleasures or risk losing everything worthwhile in my life.

"Getting away from Oliver before you do something that you'll regret," Tony said, letting the grin slip away. "You were ready to tear him to shreds, and however much you might have enjoyed it at the moment, you would have regretted it later."

I used anger to cover the shock at hearing him echoing my thoughts. "They can all go screw themselves," I said. "If Oliver ever loved my mother, I never saw it. All he wants is her money, and he'll get it. The rest of those vultures care more about their gossip. They've never cared about me. I was the 'failure' they all had to endure."

Tying off his laces, Tony hobbled over to me and sat down, using his hand to lift my chin so I could look into his eyes. "I know all about being the 'black sheep,' remember? Just ask my Dad." His eyes grew distant, and he smiled. "Oh, the things I've done to make him pull his hair out. I can't imagine a nice girl like you even being in my league."

There was a shot of genuine humor and amazement. I tried to restrain it, but the laughter took on a life of its own, and I couldn't stop. Then, when I couldn't breathe, I laughed.

When I managed to control it, I saw him smiling at me. I shook my head. "You do not know. Unless you're a lot wilder than I think you are, I can top your antics on your best day."

"We'll see. After we skate a bit, we'll have lunch - on me and we'll trade war stories," he said as he stood up, helping me to my feet. I prayed I didn't fall too often. It had been twenty years since I'd last been on skates, and I didn't want a sore butt.

Taking advantage of his help, I stumbled onto the ice and moved. He skated backward in front of me as though he were just out for a stroll.

"You're doing great," he encouraged.

"I haven't fallen and been cut to sausage," I said, windmilling my arms to keep what little balance I had. Then an eight-yearold menace blew past me at warp four, dressed from head to toe in blinding fuchsia. At this rate, I'd be lucky to survive.

"Graceful, I'm not. How did I let you talk me into this hare-brained idea?"

"It's my smooth negotiating skills."

"Hah! You threw me over your shoulder and carried me off,"

I objected. "How smooth is that?"

"You're here, aren't you?" he asked with another innocent grin. "There's an old saying, 'if it works, it isn't stupid.'

Following that logic, I think I was smooth enough."

It was hard to argue with that. Screw it. Since I was here, I might as well have a good time.

Chapter Eight

For an hour, Tony taught me how to skate all over again. He was so close I could feel the heat of his body as he showed me how to move. I tried telling myself that it wasn't doing anything to me, but I hadn't been that good at lying to myself since I was a teen. It slung-shot my hormones like a teenage boy watching Gal Gadot as Wonder Woman.

I was exhausted when we were ready to get off the ice. I'd traded my worries about the funeral for concern about falling flat on my dignity and what I was getting myself into with Tony. Every touch of his hands and body made the next contact seem less intrusive and more welcome. I wondered if that was how one tamed a wild horse. Did you touch it until it was used to your hands, caress it until I wanted more? It, I told myself, not I. That was an embarrassing slip to make, even in my mind. Caress it until it wants more.

I sighed in resignation. This was getting more complicated, and I was losing control of where it was going. Already, I felt some connection between us that was nebulous and hard to describe. Disturbing, too. I couldn't quite put my finger on it.

We turned in our skates and walked to the car. The sky was darker than earlier, and the snow was coming down more heavily.

Tony took my keys out of my hand and jumped into the driver's seat with a possessive grin. I shook my head and smiled, taking the passenger seat. When we were secure, he took off in an almost uncontrolled spin.

I squeaked and grabbed the dashboard, glaring at him. "Tony! You stop that this very second!"

He laughed but slowed down and brought the SUV under control. "Yes, Ma'am."

"Men! You're all just little boys under the skin."

Tony didn't go for the bait and drove until we pulled into a Pizza Hut.

I looked at him with a raised eyebrow as he parked the car. "Pizza Hut, is your idea of a romantic lunch?"

He smiled back at me and opened his door. "I just said lunch. Romantic is your add-on. Thanks for the insight, though. I promise I'll start thinking."

I cursed under my breath as I climbed out and strolled to the back of the vehicle. Where had that come from? He was right. He'd never said a romantic lunch, but somehow that's what it had morphed into in my mind when I wasn't thinking about it.

So what was I doing to myself this time?

We shed our coats and hung them when we got inside, and then a hostess led us to a booth. I had a tall glass of iced tea and the promise of a hot pepperoni pizza to hold my grumbling stomach at bay.

Tony sat across from me, watching me as if he expected me to say something. I didn't know what that might be, so I smiled and stared back at him. Then, after a minute, it started becoming almost comical.

I couldn't take it and shook my head. "We're just silly," I told him. "I think we had a miscue somewhere."

"Maybe," he agreed. "I don't believe in rushing things faster than they need to go, so let's just forget the word romantic for now."

I let my breath out with a sigh of relief. "Thank you. I'm not ready for that yet." Yet? I winced. What the hell possessed me to add that very word?

Tony's eyes twinkled at me, but he let it go. "So, we've talked about our childhood. What did the next twenty years bring you?"

I snorted. "Nothing but trouble. Ten years in the Army, two nasty ex-husbands, a lifetime full of regrets, and many people I've hurt or disappointed over the years."

"Come on," he said, frowning, "it can't have been that bad."

I laughed. "Oh yes, it could."

He drew me into talking about college and leaving Idaho for UCLA with brief nods and an excited expression. Again, I found myself amazed at the things I told him. We only knew each other, and I complained about how my ex-husbands were like my father. I even told him about some of the higher and lower points of my days in pre-med, including Daniel.

"So, you're a doctor?" he asked.

I shook my head. "No. I didn't want to be one. That was for Dad." At least, that was part of the story. Having seen a proper doctor up close and personal, I had realized that I'd never had the drive to be one. So I became a nurse and medic and ended up being a Captain.

Tony didn't dwell on that. "This Daniel guy sounds like an actual piece of work," he said with a scowl, "though I can't throw stones. I've had my share of relationships, but I've never been married." He said that he was too uncooperative for any woman to want. "I'm too much of a pirate."

That grin did things to my insides that I forced aside. Instead, I reminded myself I needed another man, like another hole in my head.

Using my confused state against me, he kept digging. "So, with all that behind you, what do you do to stay busy now?

I ignored his question and smirked at him. "Don't I get to ask questions about your mysterious past?"

"It's polite to talk about the lady on a date," he said.

"Is this a date?" I asked, my eyebrows rising almost against my will.

"You're the one who said it was a romantic lunch. We can quibble about the details later," he said, his tone dismissive. "Back to you."

I shook my head but smiled. "I do charity work." I launched into my list of charities I raised money for.

Tony listened and nodded. The slight frown between his eyes made me wonder if I'd said something wrong.

"That's a lot of charity work," he agreed, "but are you satisfied? What do you do for yourself? You know, to feel you've made a personal impact."

I blinked in surprise. "What? Of course, I'm satisfied with it. What gives you the idea I'm not?" Well, I wasn't happy.

I'd have been happier if I had gone to work at the Veterans Administration. But my parents didn't go for that, and my Dad said no.

The pizza disrupted my rising anger, and I forced myself back from letting the emotion overtake me before I could think.

Once Tony had a few bites inside, leaving a cheese string on his chin, he continued.

"I hear how much money you've raised, but it doesn't seem like you're getting much personal satisfaction from it," he added before I could object. "Giving money to charities helps people, but it's not very personal. That always seemed to me like helping the hypothetical needy."

What did that mean? I let the silence drag on as I thought about it and picked. He didn't interrupt me.

When I kept running into brick walls of incomprehension, I looked back up and shrugged. "I must miss something. What are you getting at? I'm satisfied with it." At least the thinking had derailed my initial angry reaction.

"Have you ever served food in a soup kitchen or helped a stranger because it made you feel good?"

I stared at him, confused. "Why would I do that when I can fund an entire kitchen? My money works much harder than I ever could by myself. I assure you I help plenty of needy people."

I didn't want him to know I did work in a soup kitchen when they didn't have enough people to show up. Tony didn't need to know that. That is my business and not his or my parents'.

Tony shrugged. "Maybe it's just me. I enjoy getting my hands dirty. Things like Habitat for Humanity build houses for people that couldn't afford to build or buy their own. My satisfaction comes from seeing them come home for the first time. Nothing beats that feeling. That lets me use the skills I learned for work to help others."

I heard what he was saying, but I didn't see how the two were different. So instead, I changed the subject by zeroing in on his work. "Speaking of your work, do you work around here, or do you travel?"

His smile told me he saw through my conversational shift but switched topics. "I travel every few months; when one project doesn't need me anymore, I go to one that does. Not just in this state, but all over the general area."

"You said you'd never married, but what about other longterm relationships?" I asked. Apart from me, I wasn't sure what I wanted to hear him say.

"Some," he admitted. "They never lasted, though. We just never seemed to mesh."

"I'm sure you'll find the right woman one day."

He nodded, his eyes dark and expressive. "I think you're right. Timing is everything."

I felt a shiver of something I didn't understand and looked at my watch. "Look at the time! We need to get a move on." His expression told me I wasn't fooling anyone. Still, it was already late in the afternoon, and I needed to return to the funeral home.

While he paid for lunch, I went to the ladies' room and scrubbed my hands across my face. What was wrong with me? Maybe I should give in and have a fling with him because this itch was getting very distracting. I shook my head at my reflection in the mirror. I didn't do casual. When the little devil's voice told me I should think about making it more than simple, I covered my eyes and groaned. I didn't need this!

I washed my hands and composed myself. The woman sitting next to the bathroom made me stop as I came out. Or rather, what she was saying into her cell phone made me stop. She was younger than me and very pregnant. She was also slumped over the table with her face buried in one hand.

"I don't know what to do, Mom," she said. "He took everything. He quit his job and just took off with everything.

No one knows where he went." Then her voice took on a bitter tone. "What everyone knows is who he ran off with. Why couldn't they have bothered to tell me before he left me like this?"

Smothering a dark and knowing smile, I slipped back into the bathroom. I listened to her through the open door. I could have told her some places to call to get help, but she seemed too proud to take advantage of them. Her pain bothered me. I didn't want to leave her in despair.

"I know you can't help me very much," she continued, "But can you wire me just a little? Fifty dollars? Oh, thank you!" She sounded almost pathetically grateful. "I'll pay you back as soon as I can. I've got a week before the landlord comes looking for the rent, and that'll buy me food and give me some gas money so I can find a job."

I blanched. Dear God, she didn't need to be working. She looked like she was due any day. She needed to be off her feet. "No," the woman said with a bit of heat. "I can't come home. He's still there, but I love you. I can't live with him. I just can't. I'd rather starve. Please try to understand."

What about her baby? Her following comment told me I wasn't the only one asking that question.

"I have little choice, do I?" she said. "As soon as he's born, I'll take him to the fire station or give him up for adoption. I don't want to, but I can't afford to keep him. He deserves better than me," she said, almost in tears.

My heart ached. She sounded like me, but I wanted to help her. I'd never had a baby, and I doubted I ever would, but her plight still struck a chord in me. I thought. What could I do?

"Yes," she continued. "Please wire it to me at the Western Union office on Main Street. And if you send him to do it, could you make sure he at least spells my name, right?" She spelled out Williamson. "At least he remembered Joan last time," she said tiredly. Then she slowly recited her address. I repeated it silently while I set my purse on the counter and dug through it, looking for something to write on. The first thing I found was Tony's card with his number. That was ironic.

I counted out what I had in cash, which totaled almost four hundred dollars. Not very much, but I paid for stuff with my card. It would just have to do.

Now I just had to figure out how to give it to her without her being able to turn me down. I folded the bills up and walked out of the bathroom. She was listening to her mother and still had her face buried in her hand, her elbow propped up on the table. Her purse was beside her elbow. I could see her loose change purse inside it. She was probably using the change for the call. I deftly dropped the bills into her bag and walked out.

Tony had the SUV idling by the curb. I climbed in, feeling light inside. I grinned at him. Who said I didn't know how to get personal satisfaction?

Everyone had deserted the funeral home by the time we arrived. All the family was gone, even Oliver. That made me boil inside. How dare they leave her like this?

I went to stand beside my mother. Looking down at her, I realized how badly having them leave her here alone hurt me. After tomorrow, I'd never see her again. That brought on a fresh onslaught of tears.

I'm not sure how long I stood there holding her hand. Feeling like every tear that fell made me somehow emptier inside when I felt someone beside me. Then I looked up, ready to chew off Oliver's head for bothering me again if he'd dared to come back, and only cut off my attack when I saw it was Tony. "Sophia, the viewing is over, and it's time to leave," he whispered. Were construction workers supposed to be gentle? They should be challenging and decisive, sure, but gentle?

"I'm not going," I said with a willful toss of my head. "I'm staying here with Mother."

I expected a condescending smile, but he didn't smile at all.

He just nodded. "I know, but you can't. We have to go."

"She's my mother, and I won't leave her," I shouted, angry with him. "I won't! She needs me here!" I waited for him to either walk away or counterattack, glad for the outlet for my pain.

Our standoff was interrupted when two police officers stopped at the parlor and came up to me, "My name is Officer Miller, and we have the warrant to take Phoebe Masterson's body into custody."

I wasn't breathing. I know because I can usually feel it, even hear it at times of great excitement or intense stress. So why can't I listen to it? Tony's construction worker's hands were the only things between me and a carpet needing vacuuming.

The look of indifference on the face of the massive man in uniform told me I wouldn't get any sympathy. "What... did you say? And... and why did you say it?" Then, Officer Miller stepped forward with his blank blue eyes, receding hairline, and a coffee-stained shirt half a doughnut away from popping two buttons. "While Ms. Masterson's body was at the M.E.'s lab, a pre-med bonehead assistant was supposed to take a blood sample from a different body but pricked her's instead. That sample was sent off, and it was discovered that there was a deadly amount of poison in her system."

Officer Miller put his hand on my mom's casket, probably to hold himself up. "It wasn't cancer that killed this woman; it was murder."

Chapter Nine

"Murder?" I exclaimed. Tony redoubled his efforts to keep me upright. "Who would...."

"Who are you?" Officer Miller's question, as well as his suspicious glare, was direct.

"I'm Sophia Thomas, Phoebe's daughter," I replied coldly. My shock was becoming apparent. Tony helped me to a nearby chair. It wasn't cancer. It wasn't Goddamn cancer. She could be home right now. She could have been with me. We could be toasting every asshole we ever met. She could be telling me I'm okay, that everything will be okay. She.... Who would do this?

Officer Miller cleared, "This is routine, but can you tell me where you were on the night of your mother's death?"

"I was at a charity auction and dance. It was televised in San Francisco for the police department," I said, with an accent on the last part. "I got there at four to set up and didn't leave until three. Although, before you ask, I was on stage most of the night and getting things for everyone." I pulled out a card that had the information of whom they could get ahold of to verify I was there all night. Luckily, they found it necessary to talk to the man I was in bed with that night.

"Where can we find Mr. Masterson?" Officer Miller asked.

"Knowing him, he's at home, probably sitting in his thousanddollar recliner he brought himself for Father's day because he knew I wouldn't; honestly, I'm not sure where he is." I thought he would be here."

The screaming was in my head. The part of me that wanted to run and never stop was at odds with the other factor that stood motionless as the EMTs took my mother's body out of the coffin. He placed her on a gurney, then covered her face before rolling her out the door. While seated, Tony's hands were still on my shoulders. I told myself it was for comfort, but I wanted to jump out of the chair and go after the cops. Tony knew it. I tried to shove him away, but he was too strong. "Let me go!" I wailed. "Just leave me alone!" "No," was the reply.

As quickly as it arrived, the anger fled my body. I felt grief for my loss, and a deep and abiding fear of never seeing my mother again flooded through me; someone killed my mom. "I don't want her to go," I cried, clutching him. "Please, don't let them take her."

"I know this is hard for you," he whispered, "but she's already gone."

I sobbed, half-broken away from him, and started pounding my fists on his chest. "Someone killed her!"

He didn't resist my attack, but it was like hitting a brick wall, except I had a better chance of knocking down the wall. When the tears pushed the anger away, he pulled me back into his arms, and this time I didn't resist. "It hurts, I know," he whispered. "But she's already gone to a better, happier place." "But I don't want her to go!"

He turned away from the casket and pulled me toward the door while I cried and railed against him. By the time he put my coat on me, all the fight had gone out of my body. I just stood there, let him slip it on, and he led me out to his Land Rover. I didn't even object when he strapped me in like a child.

Tony belted himself in and took the Rover to the street, leaving Oliver's SUV behind. "Left or right?" he prompted.

When I looked outside, snow was falling, and the wind had picked up. I took a deep breath and pulled myself together enough to give him directions out of town and up the mountain.

He didn't talk to me on the drive other than prompt me for directions. I didn't understand, but I was grateful. Weren't men supposed to fix everything? Not all of them. At least one could listen without judging. I felt wrung out. I'd lost my control and composure again, and I was glad that Oliver and Dad hadn't seen me. I couldn't do anything right, it seemed.

The interior of the Rover sank into my awareness. Tony had packed it with tools, and the Rover smelled like.... like him, I realized. It didn't smell bad, just male. I rolled my eyes and laughed inside at myself. This was just perfect. I didn't have the time or emotional energy for this.

Tony glanced at me and smiled before returning his eyes to the road in silence, giving me time to get myself back under control.

Chapter Ten

By the time we pulled up in front of the ranch, the police had come. I'd regained enough composure to get out of the Rover and wait for Tony to meet me by the door.

He had his overnight bag in hand when he joined me.

"I'm sorry," I whispered.

He gave me a throwaway gesture. "You've done nothing to be sorry about, so don't worry about it."

I smiled and nodded. "Come on inside, and let's get you settled." After taking off our shoes and coats, I led the way and gave him the same quick tour I'd given Karla yesterday. I found the police talking to my father.

"This is a nice place," he said, looking at the ceiling. "Well put together."

I stared at the ceiling, and it looked like.... a top. Please leave it to Tony to ignore the decorations and go right to the surrounding structure. "I should just start calling you Bob Vila."

He laughed. "I can't help it."

With an amused shake of my head, I took him into Oliver's hall. I found him an empty room, pointing out everything he needed to know, then excused myself.

I left him to put his things away and went to the bar. From the quiet, it was evident that Oliver, Dad, and the police were talking there, so I figured I might as well go to my room to talk to me and get ready for them. Times like these made me wish I'd never given up using coke, as much pain and loss as the stuff

had caused. I felt the siren's call of the little vial in my room, which seemed like an excellent idea. Daniel was right, I thought. I couldn't deal with this on my own.

I grabbed the box from under my bed and held another note.

March 11, 1999

Phoebe,

Hey, how's it going?

Okay, for me, I guess so. How's life for ya? All right here, except I miss Curtis.

So how was your camping trip? All right? I went camping too but to Pebble Creek. Kool-Aid, but anyway, shit, I don't know what else to say. Shit.

It's so fucking boring. There's nothing to do. I went and stole a bunch of cool pens last night... It was cool. But uh. I miss Curtis; he went fishing, but anyway. I'm going to drop. I hear because I don't know what else to say, so catch you later. Damian

I thought he didn't want to talk to mom again; that is weird, but it's high school, and you fight. So I pulled out the following note and opened it.

March 18, 1999

Damian

Hi how are You?

She might go partying with me, Jess, and Michelle tonight. Michelle's boyfriend reminds me of you. I know, fine as hell... He has a body like yours, and when I saw him, he reminded me of you. How about Curtis? Are you two back together yet? If not, don't give up. Your love will never subside, so baby, deal with it anyway. I know what it's like not to have any hope at all. Little few chances to pull strings. A kiss, a touch, a smile, a call, you know, I'm sure... Well, I guess I'll drop it here. I just thought I'd drop you a few words and say Hi.

Latter's love always,

Phoebe

P/S I got my letter today, and I will be at Fort Jackson from July

19 - Sept 26. I drilled this weekend. I'm all right. I guess just going with the flow like the sergeant said. I love it here in Boise. Poky is so lame in comparison. There are different types of people, and what have you been up to? Ross called me twice, but I haven't seen him yet. His here with me but in a different section.

I put the note back down, still at a loss as to why my mom insisted I read them; they made no sense to me. I poured myself a stiff drink, downed it, then refilled the glass. I preferred an excellent wine over liquor, but I needed something more. The burn settled in my stomach, and I relaxed. I opened the glass doors and stepped onto the snow-packed deck, taking the bottle with me. The cold burned into me, but I ignored it. I left the lights off and closed the door behind me.

The hot tub dominated the deck. I longed just to climb in and soak.

Stepping out, my bare feet crunched in the snow. I stared into the darkness and let the cold numb my feet. Then, sipping my drink, I cleared a spot on the rail and set the bottle down. It seemed impossible, but the snow was falling even more complicated now.

Even though I could only see the tops of some of the closest trees, they were right at the level of the deck. The ground behind the ranch sloped down gradually.

I felt the heat leaching from me and refilled my glass. I knew I should go back inside, but the part that didn't care seemed in control of my muscles, and I stayed there shivering in the snow. Finally, setting my glass down beside the bottle, I cleared a wider area of the rail and climbed up to sit on it with my legs dangling into the darkness below.

Here I was, alone. Not that I'd been any other way for very long. I emptied my glass and tried to refill it, but my numb fingers couldn't hold the glass, and it dropped into the abyss in front of me. It was gone as if it had never been.

Staring down, I felt a moment of vertigo and gripped the rail below me. I marveled at how easy that had been. One moment and the glass was gone. It was tumbling down the steep slope unless it had smashed into a tree. I wondered if that would hurt much. Or for long.

My dark ruminations stopped when the door to the room opened behind me. "Sophia?" Tony asked.

I thought about just pushing off. A few seconds and it would be over. They could bury me with my mother, and no one would care except for my friends.

Thinking of mom, I rejected the thought of jumping and cursed my lack of resolve as he walked up behind me. "It looks like a long way down." "It is," I assured him.

"Then let me help you back onto the deck. I don't want you to fall." He took the bottle from my hand and set it on the rail, pulling me back onto the deck with no effort. Then, standing me up in front of him, he eyed me critically. "And it's too cold out here for you to be without a jacket or shoes. Come inside, and we'll sit in front of the fireplace."

"I don't want to go in," I said petulantly. "I want to stay out here."

"If we stay out here, we need to be warmer," he said. "Let's step inside and get our coats and shoes."

So, he didn't trust me alone out here. He must have sensed something in my voice. This man was far more perceptive than I cared for right now.

"Let's get in the hot tub," I countered. "Its temperature alone is enough to keep us warm." I pulled the cover off the tub. What was I doing?

I saw him grin in the darkness. "I didn't think to bring my swimsuit with me."

I grinned back, challengingly. "I didn't either. Come on. I promise your virtue is safe with me." Had I lost my mind? Getting naked in a hot tub with a man was begging to be screwed. Silly, and I didn't know him at all. It would never work. Still, part of me whispered that getting screwed silly had its upsides.

"Sophia, you've been drinking, and you might regret..."

With a laugh, I pulled my blouse over my head and threw it to the side. "I've done so many things over the years that I regret that one more will hardly matter. You can either join me in the tub or go back inside."

He watched me strip and drop my clothes on the deck. I could see the interest on his face, even in the dark. He wasn't Superman or gay. That was a relief. I grabbed the bottle from the rail and set it on the side of the tub before stepping in. The hot water felt scalding before my body adjusted to the radical change in temperature. Finally, I settled into the water and let it flow to my neck.

With a shrug, Tony disrobed with economical movements and stepped into the tub. His torso rippled with muscle, which kicked my hormones into a higher gear. Or maybe it was his erection. It bobbed as he settled into the water. Not gay, though he sat almost out of reach.

I took a swig of liquor straight from the bottle and handed it over to him. He took a drink and set it beside him.

"I think you're too hard on yourself, but tonight isn't the right time to talk about this," he said, handing the bottle back to me. "It's never too late to start again. Who hasn't done something we'd do differently now? You can't change the past, but you can decide to live the rest of your life differently. Break the cycle." "That's easy to say," I snorted.

Tony nodded. "It's the hardest thing in the world to do. It means knowing whom we want to be and intentionally making that leap of faith to leave the old us behind forever."

I sat, mulling over the magnitude of what he'd said. Then, until he changed the subject to trivial, more mundane things, I entered, discussing what we liked and hated. We talked about food, wine, and movies. We passed the bottle back and forth. Within five minutes, a comfortable sense of familiarity had replaced the tension. Yet, the more I relaxed, the more a sense of something wrong nagged at the back of my mind.

Chapter Eleven

It took me almost an hour to figure out what was bothering me. When I finally pinned it down, I was shocked to my toes. Over the years, I'd felt a deep attachment to only a few select people. These people had become my closest and dearest friends, and it had happened in a matter of hours or days each time. First, we'd sit and talk, and then it was as if we'd known each other all our lives. In each case, we'd also become lovers soon after that.

This had nagged me since I'd met him, but I couldn't see the danger. This wasn't good. How could this have happened? I was in my mid-thirties and had never felt this way toward a man. Not even the ones I'd married. What is wrong with me? It couldn't be the booze. I'd been as drunk and high on coke countless times. This had never happened before. Now that it had, I did not know what it meant or what to do about it.

"Is something wrong?" Tony asked. He set the empty bottle outside the tub and stretched his back, causing his chest to ripple. My body reacted in a way that it shouldn't. Heat flashed back through me, and I wanted him here and now.

Even in hot water, a chill ran up my spine. I didn't understand what was happening, and I needed space. Gathering what dignity I could muster, I stood up and let the water sluice off me. I was a little unsteady, but a hand on the side of the tub allowed me to regain my balance. Tony looked at me, and I could see the desire in his eyes.

With more strength than I thought I had, I stepped out of the hot tub and started gathering my clothes. "I'm going in and showering." That sounded abrupt, and I heard a quiver in my voice that wasn't there very often. Whatever faults I had, lack of self-assurance wasn't one of them.

Tony hid the flash of disappointment well. I would have missed it if I hadn't looked right at him as he transitioned to a thoughtful nod and masked his initial reaction. I didn't think he was angry, though, like Daniel would have been. He was just disappointed. He rose from the tub, grabbed his clothes, and followed me. "Good idea. We were going to wrinkle soon."

We went our separate ways, and I left my clothes in my room before getting into the shower. I let the hot water run for a few minutes to clean and then turned it cold. The icy water shocked my body, and I hoped it would shock some sense into me and quench these feelings. I didn't have any business feeling like this toward a man.

After toweling off, I slipped on my robe and returned to my room to dress. I was surprised to find Tony sitting on the edge of the bed. I was unsure of myself. Was this the play for me I hadn't thought was coming? But, of course, he was dressed, so that didn't seem likely, but he was a man, after all.

"Your door was open, so I thought I'd wait for you here. That's a delicate piece of art," he said with a nod to the miniature painting on the wall. It was of a skier taking a slope with a spray of snow rooster-tailing behind her. "Is that you?"

I smiled but shook my head. "No, it's not me. I just saw it at an online auction and picked it up. I don't know him, but the artist does good work. Remember him if you need anything. His name is Keven Braddock, and he's in LA." I hesitated in stripping off the robe to dress but decided that was kind of idiotic after flaunting my body in front of him.

I tossed the robe onto the bed and started dressing in something casual. I could feel his eyes caressing me and cursed the flutter in my stomach. He didn't get up and try anything or make any comments. Maybe he would not try something after all.

He waited for me to dress, then pointed to the dresser. "Mind if I ask what that is?"

It took me a moment to realize what he was talking about, and then I flushed. I put the vial into my pants pocket while I struggled for some reasonable explanation. Then I sighed, damning the feeling of guilt that it caused me. I wouldn't lie to a friend like that, and this was something that could ruin our budding friendship. Well, maybe it was all for the good if it did. That would at least get me out of the uncomfortable mental place where I'd cornered myself.

"It's coke." There. There it was. I'd done it now to see where all the pieces landed, now that I'd blown everything up. I watched him with what calm I could muster.

His face expressionless, he nodded. "I thought it might be. I heard people talking at the viewing, and one of them mentioned you'd had a drug problem, but he thought you'd kicked it."

The unasked question hung in the air. Was he wrong? I shook my head. "I went through rehab. I don't feel like talking about it, but I haven't relapsed for almost five years."

"Then why relapse now? Is it because of your mom?"

I shrugged and inexplicably felt tired. Pulling the plain wooden chair over, I sat in front of Tony. "It's hard to explain. I haven't relapsed yet. Or I'm in the process of relapsing. Or I've relapsed but just haven't taken a snort yet." I had to admit that when I hadn't said no, I'd said yes. I just hadn't gotten up the nerve to snort it yet. That bastard Daniel!

"But you want to?" Tony asked quietly.

I nodded slowly. "I'm tired of being down all the time," I said, the tears starting down my face. "I can't handle this."

Tony took my hands in his. "I assume you quit for a reason the last time because it was messing up your life. Right?"

I laughed. "You say that as if you haven't heard all the rumors. I swear, I hate having relatives."

He shot a crooked smile at me. "I try not to hold past inappropriate behavior against anyone. Glass houses and wrecking balls, you understand. I won't say something stupid like 'it doesn't matter,' but it's irrelevant. I've only known you a little while, but I can see something worthwhile inside you. Something honorable."

I snorted and shook my head. "You don't have my reputation."

"No, I have my own," he admitted. "But that isn't what I'm getting at. Let me put it this way. Paraphrasing Lois McMaster Bujold, a science fiction author, *Reputation is what other people know about you. Honor is what you know about yourself.* Our stress about it happens when the two aren't the same. So be true to yourself and the hell with what everyone else thinks."

He smiled at my startled expression. "Look, the past is just that: the past. It's the road we walked to get where we are, not who we are. If you don't like where you are, all you have to do to change is walk away. As hard as that can sometimes be." He pointed to my pocket. "I will ask: will that help you a week from now or hurt you?"

Bowing my head, I swallowed. "When I'm high, I don't feel bad, but it takes over my life. I'd have to say that coke helped push college and my first marriage to slow destruction. It took me falling apart and a good friend intervening to force me to get help. Emma kept at me until I couldn't deny it anymore.

Then she stood by me and watched me like a hawk for months."

"That's an actual friend," he agreed. "I'm surprised she isn't here now."

"I wish she were," I sighed, looking back into his compassionate eyes. "She's out of the country."

"If you haven't relapsed in five years, where did you get the coke? In town?"

"No. Daniel gave it to me."

"Daniel?" he asked with a frown. "Your ex-boyfriend? He lives here?"

"God, no," I said with some heat. "He flew in for the funeral. So he's staying in the room next to mine."

Tony's eyes hardened. "He came in and dangled that in front of you at a time like this?"

I shrugged. "Yeah."

With a visible effort, he brought himself back under control. "I don't think you should give up. That's what giving in would be. I don't think you're a quitter, Sophia. Since your friend isn't here, let me step into her shoes." His eyes bored into mine. "You don't need that crutch. I'm here for you, and I'll stay right here as long as you need me. That's going to tempt you every minute you keep it. Dump it. If you can't do that just for yourself, do it for your friend Emma and me. Please."

The indecision tore at me.

Finally, I nodded, dug the vial out of my pocket, and tossed it onto the bed beside him. "You're right. Get rid of it."

When he shook his head, I stared in surprise and incomprehension. He picked up the vial and held it out. "You need to get rid of it, I think. Don't let someone else do it for you."

I didn't know whether to laugh, cry, or get angry. "Why?"

"Because if you pass it off to me, that's passing off the responsibility for your life to me. I want you to dump it. Take responsibility for your own life."

Taking the vial in my hand, I stood up on unsteady feet. Tony rose with me and followed me into the bathroom, where I unscrewed the cap and tried to force my hand to dump it into the toilet. Then, I tossed it into the water, after a moment where I thought I would not do it.

"Flush it," he commanded.

With the plunge of the handle, the coke was gone. I screwed the lid back on the empty vial and clutched it. Tony pulled me into his arms and held me as I wept softly.

"It's going to be okay," he whispered. Then, when the tears slowed and my nose stuffed up, he walked me back to my room. He pried the empty vial from my hand and set it on the dresser before finding me some tissues.

He let me dry my tears and regain my composure in companionable silence. I knew he wanted to talk more, but he didn't rush me. I appreciated that.

The slam of the front door interrupted any further opportunity to talk. I jumped a little, opened the door to my bedroom, and listened to see who was home. When I heard no voices, I stood up and debated closing the door. However, I froze when Daniel approached the door and straight in.

"Hey, Babe, I..." he drew up short when he saw Tony standing by the bed. "Who are you?" he demanded.

Tony said nothing, but his body language was crystal clear. Gone was the gentleman who had helped me get a grip on my life, and in his place stood an angry man. A dangerous man, his eyes so soft toward me, were now chips of flint ready to spark a fire. I decided I had to act before he did something I wouldn't regret.

"His name is Tony," I said with a cold toss of my head. I stood up and pointed to the door. "But I don't recall inviting you in, Daniel, so hit the road."

Still glaring at Tony, Daniel's eyes flicked around the room, and I saw the hidden gleam when he saw the empty vial. His expression made me look down in shame that I'd almost succumbed to it and him. "I just came in to talk about the weather, Babe. No need to get all huffy. The snow has been falling nonstop."

Tony stepped in front of me.

"She said to go," he said. "You can either go on your own, or I'll toss your sorry ass out."

"I can handle him, Tony," I said as I gathered my anger. "We're done, Daniel. Get out." My stuffed nose ruined my imperious tone.

He smiled at me and strolled out the door, laughing. “You know where to find me if you want to talk about the weather.”

Tony closed the door behind him and locked it. Then he took me into his arms. “I should’ve beat the shit out of him.”

I smiled. “That’d be a horrible idea,” I said. “Dad likes him. I think Daniel is the son he never had. I have to live under the same roof as him.”

“No, you don’t,” he whispered. “Come away with me.”

My head came up, and I searched his face, trying to decide what he meant by that. Part of me struggled to shake my head and refuse, but another part was more vital and melted into his arms, and I nodded. “Where will we go?”

His hand tilted my face to look into my eyes. “I still have the room I booked for tonight and tomorrow. We can share it.” He must have seen the struggle in my heart because he covered my lips with his fingers. “No obligations. I promise that I’ll be a gentleman.”

A growing part of me didn’t want him to be a gentleman, but I was grateful not to have to decide now while I was upset.

“Okay. Let me pack a bag.”

“I’ll be back in a minute after I grab my stuff. Don’t open the door unless you hear me outside.” I thought he would kiss me for a second, and I trembled, but he let me go.

After he left, I locked the door and started packing. I debated what to take and decided to take what I needed for a few days. Screw the rest. My emotions were wooden at first, but as I packed, I gained resolution, and my actions became faster and firmer.

I was still gathering my makeup when I heard a knock at the door. I dropped my bag, and my heart pounded.

“Sophia,” Tony called through the door, “Open up.”

I unlocked the door and stared at him. “You scared the hell out of me!”

He laughed. “Sorry. Are you ready?”

"Give me a second." I picked my bag back up, swept my makeup inside, and zipped it. "Now I am," grabbing the box with the notes and handing them to Tony.

"What's the box for?" Tony asked.

"My mom gave me goodbye letters, and they're all in the box," I said.

He didn't waste time asking me if I was sure. Good. When he started, I followed him. The great room showed no sign of Daniel, so either he'd left again or was in his room. Even better. I wondered where everyone else was as we put on our outerwear. Then I decided I didn't care.

The only cars outside were Tony's Land Rover, and the rental Mercedes was Daniel's. There was still no sign of the police, Oliver, or Dad. Excellent.

Chapter Twelve

A few false turns and half an hour later, we were at the Doubletree. I looked over the lounge. It wasn't the Waldorf, but it would do. I followed him to the room when he was done, and it looked adequate, if small. It would be fine for sleeping. Then it hit me. The room was single. I turned to look at Tony with a quirked eyebrow.

He shrugged and set his bag on the floor. "I expected to be alone when I reserved it. Don't worry; I'll sleep in the chair." He gestured at the uncomfortable-looking padded chair in the corner.

"If you say you'll behave, I believe you," I said with a shake of my head, setting my bag on the low-slung dresser and the box on the bee. "The bed is enormous enough for us to sleep without trouble."

"I don't want to make you feel uncomfortable," he whispered, opening the bag and moving his clothes and gear into one side of the dresser.

"That's sweet, but I won't. If I do, you'll know it." I unpacked and loaded half of the dresser with clothes.

After we'd hung up the clothes that needed hanging and put our toiletries into the bathroom, I sat on the bed. I wondered where this unexpected relationship was going. Then I shook my head. No, there was no relationship. None.

"Hungry?" Tony asked. "We can order room service."

"Not really," I said, "but don't let me stop you if you are. I'm all worn out."

"Then let's just get some sleep," he suggested. "I'll ask for a wake-up call while you get ready for bed."

"Who do you think killed my mom?" I asked.

"I don't know, but something is wrong with your family," Tony said.

I walked into the bathroom, brushed my teeth, and weighed my options. Part of me still wanted to go back into the bedroom and shake the growing lust I was feeling. If it had been a woman instead of Tony, I would have indulged, but I still felt held back. Staring at myself in the mirror, I shook my head. If I gave in to my desire, it would be for more than a piece of ass, and I still couldn't believe I felt this intensity in such a short time. I needed to sleep on it.

When I was done, I let him have the bathroom and pulled out a long t-shirt to wear over my panties. I turned off all the lights except for the lamp by my side of the bed. I settled in between the sheets and listened to him brush his teeth. This domestication came from nowhere and made me feel something I hadn't felt in a long time. Lonely.

I grabbed the box and opened an additional note.

July 30, 1999

Phoebe

When you left, I should have never broken up with you. I just wanted you to know that I love you. I need your help to decide what I'm going to do. I wish you'd wait for a little longer. You just left for basic. You joined, and I still can't believe it. What were you thinking? I don't want you to go. You know what it was like when I was grounded. Without me, you did everything to see me. It was only for a couple of weeks, but you still caught me a lot. Once you're gone, you're gone. I won't see you at home, school, shower, or anywhere. No one will be there to rush me along in the morning. In the morning, to teach me how to get laid. To give me her science to copy. To scratch your back, I guess your back won't need to be scratched, huh? Haha, a poor joke?

Please wait, Phoebe. I can't handle it right now; It will fuck me up. Not now. Please, someday, we'll get our licenses, and then we can do it together. Thelma and Louise. We'll drive off a cliff. But please hold on a little longer. I'll fall apart. I love you too much, and I can't handle it. Please give it one more chance? I love you. What the hell is our song? I have so much more to talk to you about. There's not enough time. I wouldn't say I like summer school. I love you. I love you. I love you. I'm sorry about everything. I'm sorry for being annoying and slow. I love you, and thank you for teaching me how to fuck, taking me under your wing, and letting me invade your living space and buy my fries.

I'll write back.

Damian

I folded the letter up and put it in the box. I pushed back the feelings of warmth that his ordinary preparations for bed had raised. How had he managed to get through all my defenses with such ease?

I was still stewing in that hot soup of emotion when Tony came out of the bathroom in a pair of tight briefs and an undershirt. Somehow, seeing him like that was much more erotic than seeing him naked. I smiled and patted the bed beside me without a word.

When he was under the covers, I looked into his eyes and leaned forward until our lips touched, and I kissed him softly for a moment. If he'd kissed me back and wanted more, I would've given myself to him, but he let me pull back without acting on the arousal I could see in his eyes.

"What's in the box?" Tony asked.

"My mom wanted me to read these notes to tell a family secret. So far, I've read five to six of the notes. This guy, my mom, is dating is not the best. It looks like he got her into drugs for a while and sneaked out of the house and so on," I said.

"Why don't you read one out loud?" Tony asked.

"Okay, I can understand that my mom was dating Damian, and Damian was also dating a guy named Curtis. So he got her into drugs for a little while. Then my mom joined the National Guard and went to Basic her junior year before starting last year of school," I said, grabbing another note and opening it.

August 10, 1999

Damian,

Hey babe, what are you up to? Not a lot, just sitting in algebra class and writing you a note. I just got a letter from Katie. I guess she doesn't want to hear any more about it. I need to know whether you got her pregnant while I was in Basic or before I left. I know you said they could all fuck themselves. Curtis is in my next hour. I can't wait to see what he says, anyway. I wanted you to know that I love and trust you, okay. I believe you when you say you were not with her. Right now, I have no doubts, but once I talk to Kris, who knows. But. I might if she lies to my face. I'll be pissed, but if I find out you've lied to my face, I'll be even more pissed. But I guess we will see, uh? But I trust you, and I love you, Damian.

Well, see you,

Love always, Phoebe

"Should I read one more?" I asked.

"Go ahead. This is interesting," Tony said.

August 15, 1999

Phoebe

High! What are you doing? Me, nothing much, just sitting here thinking about you. I wish I could see you right now. I miss you. So how was summer school today? This is a strange day, even weird.

Anyhow, I wouldn't say I like Curtis. He is such a fucken hypocrite. I heard some shit about that punk. I don't know who the hell he thinks he's fooling? Me, uh Bitch. God, I hate him. So guess what?

My dad will give me the money to buy that CD tomorrow, cool. Payday.

Yes, I love those days. I can see you having a smoke well. I talked to Katy. Everything is excellent. I guess too bad you can't come over. I miss ya. Maybe you can convince your mom by letting her know I'm going to get the CD tomorrow, uh?.

I must apologize too. Shit, But I hate your mom. Damn, you look fine from here, too. I only have to talk to Joe; it's no piece of cake. I don't give a fuck about Curtis. He can fuck himself for all I care. He always does, anyway. So I better drop it here, but always remember I love you.

Damian

I just met Tony. We shared a ride, a meal, my grief, my past, and now a purely platonic bed, but we had just met. I can't read him. He has already shown that he doesn't think or react like most men, so I can't read him. Did he think this was ridiculous, but he's just being nice? A gentleman?

"Have you searched his name, maybe to see where he is now? The guy in the letter," Tony asked. After a pause, I picked up my cell phone and looked up his information. It made for some interesting, if not disturbing, reading. I discovered he spent some time in prison and is a registered sex offender. Tony sat very close as he looked over my shoulder, reading what I was reading. Finally, we turned to each other before returning the letter to the box.

"Thank you for listening," I whispered and turned out the light.

The warmth of his body next to mine relaxed me in a way I never would've imagined. However, it also kept me awake long past the start of his soft snores, thinking - debating with myself. A smile crept across my face.

I was thinking about him and wondering what I had thanked him for when sleep took me.

Chapter Thirteen

I woke up slowly, luxuriating in comfortable warmth. Then I realized I was half-sprawled across someone. A man, Tony, my suddenly awake brain, informed me. His scent filled my senses, with my face buried in his hair and my lips brushing his neck.

The rest of my body began reporting, and the news went downhill. Finally, my thigh rested on an aroused cock, and his arm was between us, cupping one of my breasts through my tee shirt. Unconsciously, I began gently moving against him. Then my forebrain caught up with my hindbrain and froze my hips. This was not what I wanted.

Liar.

I lifted my head a little to look at his sleeping face. I wanted to kiss those soft lips again, and I couldn't keep fooling myself about not liking him. Now, with that out of the way, I just needed to decide whether I would give in to my desires.

I was still wrestling with myself when the phone rang. Tony's eyes popped open, and we stared at each other from a few inches away. I could see his eyes flicker with surprise at the sudden realization that I was lying primarily on top of him. Then the alarm realized he had an excellent morning erection rubbing my inner thigh and breast in his hand. I felt my nipple stiffen against his palm through the cloth of my t-shirt.

The phone rang a few more times while he got his brain in gear, pulled his hand away from my breast, and answered the

phone. Finally, a murmur told me it was our wake-up call. When he hung up, I started to swoop in to take a kiss, but he beat me to it, kissing me softly and pulling back from me.

"Sorry," he said, rearranging his briefs as he stood up. "I didn't intend to grope you." He looked embarrassed, and I realized he had taken his promise to behave very seriously.

"We were asleep. You did nothing I'm objecting to," I whispered. I took a deep breath and let it out. "Tony, I want you. And that scares me."

The spark in his eyes was impossible to miss. "Don't be scared. The feelings are mutual. However," he said regretfully as he climbed out of bed, "Is there going to be a funeral today?"

"I don't know," grabbing my cell and looking at the text that read: *Funeral today, your mom's body will not be there.* Dad wrote. *This way, people will not have to stay longer. Don't cause trouble today. Understand.* I showed the text to Tony.

"We must get a move on, or we'll be late," Tony said.

With a nod, I slipped out of bed. "Do you want to shower first?"

"We could shower together," he suggested, pulling me closer with a hand on my hip.

"Not if we want to get to the funeral home on time," I said. "Go shower."

I brushed my teeth and sat on the toilet listening to him shower while wracking my brain on how to proceed. The speed and force of my emotions made me feel out of control again. I shouldn't have told him I wanted him. That gave him power over me; I didn't know if any man could be trusted with that control.

I looked at the box and pulled out another note. I didn't understand mom and these notes, but I'm happy to do what she asked one last time.

October 30, 1999,

Phoebe,

My love of a lifetime. Hi baby, how's it going? Alright, for me, when I'm with you, but when Curtis is around....

I feel stupid, embarrassed, and just plain sad. Only because I can't look into his eyes anymore. I don't know, though. I'll do anything. When he's around, it sucks, and it's way fucking complicated. I wish he never used the word goodbye still; I hate those fucking words, but everything would be much better. None of that shit we all went through would have ever come close to happiness. Ya agree? If he wants to be with me, I can't let you hurt him again, Phoebe. I don't know what I'm going to do. It's a way big decision. I must make it hurt nobody. I can't see either of you broke again. I can't ever see Curtis again. We've suffered too much hurt and pain in the last year and two months. I can't see it anymore. I can't even look into his eyes. So, I sure in the hell can't see him hurt anymore. I can't hurt you again. I did too much in the past. I promise you, Jill, and I will try hard this time not to. You want to stick to those who I promised. If I broke my promise to myself, I would be hurt too. I'd be crushed. Just like that, I asked you out, and I don't want to break up with you because I know how you feel. I feel the same way too. I also have a lot of feelings for Curtis, but they are way more potent for Curtis. Never again could I love like that. Never. I promise to cause it is how I feel, and he hurt me so much. My feeling sunk into my heart forever and will never die. Honest.

I will never forget Curtis; my feelings will stay the same and never change until I die. I promise that too! To me, that's true love in my eyes. Maybe not in others, but I experienced the drama nobody else did. Only me and I knew the whole truth about the brief romance, and it was love at first sight, and we went through a lot of shit together. I will never forget them. That is what all the pictures are for. To help you, remind you about the boy that loved you and cared for you so much. The boy who loved a boy of the same sex and stuck by me through a lot of shit. I will never forget Curtis if I live for eternity or, better yet, infinity. I know every chance.

He can tell me not to get him again. All he wants is cozy. Next time I will have the same chance. But, of course, always fifty/fifty even. I, of course, it is not comfortable for me. Remember you and Jill never part from each other for as long as we live? We're going to get our own house and everything.

Whether we were friends or not, we'd always be together forever. I could never forget all we've been through, either. So many memories come back again. It will stay in our hearts, but I'm going to admit I have second thoughts about that boy, but I'm concerned about you. I would have let you down and my hopes and dreams to handle it. Until I die, I will be in a strait jacket. But I can't let myself or Jill down, either. I've walked and let someone walk alone with me, and it hurts to cheat yourself and lie when you already know what's happening.

Just because you don't care about yourself and treat people better and even let them kill you, I also would break promises I made I could never die, especially cause they're with me, you, and Jill. Never will I break them. It hurts, too, Goddamn bad. I've been in the position and felt the hurt, pain, and suffering that almost killed me. I've realized getting hurt is deadly, so I'll never hurt anybody again. I can't do that to you ever.

We both wouldn't be able to suicide out of the world. We've both experienced pressures to end it all, and we should have let someone run our life by trying to commit suicide together that night, but it didn't work. So we might as well get some stupid ass reason for something foolish and kill ourselves. If we let our close people run our lives like that...No, we don't need friends like that. It would have been stupid if we died, but we could have done it for a good cause.

I appreciate it and will never forget that you saved my life two weeks ago for this boy, who didn't even stay true to me. He lied to me about everything and how he felt for me—leaving me in pain and suffering to end it all. You got me help, and I was dumb for doing it.

I had to get that out for so long, but not to his face. But I could go on about another two pages, but I'm in a hurry. But I'll catch your fine ass later, Baby. Get better. You look sick or something; it's fucking scaring me.

Love you always and forever Damian

It isn't easy to read Damian's letters. He's so incomprehensible. He's probably high as my mom's handwriting that was attached stoned most of the time. But a note in my mom's handwriting was attached to the end of this letter.

Phoebe,

Please keep reading. You will understand everything if you keep reading. All these letters have a meaning you need to understand.

I promise,

Love,

Mom

I heard Tony turn off the shower and climb out with water streaming down his body. His wet hair clung to his neck and shoulders, and he looked like some Greek God. The Sophia of twenty years ago would have thrown him against the wall - at least she would have if he had been a woman - funeral service be damned. But I'd learned to restrain myself—most of the time. Restraint still didn't stop the wave of lust that rolled up my body and lit me on fire. "Reading more letters?" Tony asked.

"Yes, you can read this, and I'll jump in the shower." Pulling my eyes from Tony, I stepped into the shower. The washing ritual brought me some control, and I felt much better when I climbed out and dried off.

"Holy shit! Why is your mom making you read these letters?" Tony asked from outside the door.

"I have no clue why. If you want, you can read all the ones I've read," I said, walking out as Tony put his tie on when I came in and laid out the dress I'd picked for the funeral. I sat down and reached for my makeup but stopped when I saw my hand trembling badly. If I tried to apply makeup while shaking like this, I'd look like an extra from a slasher movie. I couldn't look like that in front of Mother. But I couldn't disappoint Dad.

Tony put his hands on my trembling shoulders. "You can do this," he said. "Take one step at a time and put one foot in front of the other. Then, I'll read the next note out loud to you if you want."

I smiled wanly and nodded. "It's going to be the hardest thing I've done to read. Maybe it was high, maybe my mom for a long time, but with you behind me, I might live through it. Of course, you can read the next note out loud if you want. But, I warn you, Damian's letters can be hard."

He kissed my cheek and backed off. I was going to the box, grabbing the following letter.

November 3, 1999

Phoebe,

How are you doing today? I'm hanging out. Did you know it's the devil's night? Oh well, what am I supposed to do? I've tried everything possible, but I have nothing else to do. So I guess I say, oh well. I'm happy.

I want to stay with you and live all the time happily. Not parttime, but all the time. I'm sick of always being part-time. Should we be lovers? I'm tired of being the person he tells or says he still loves, but he won't do anything about it. Except fucking with my head and still trying to make me believe he knows me. I'd end up feeling just 'cause I'm so dense, and I'm going to tell him as I told you. I'm like he told you. I'm sick of waiting around when he's got his mind, but he doesn't. He thinks he loves me, and he wants me. He's tired of my fucken hand that leaves sores on his dick. He's just a sick little fuck, anyway. Masturbating, little bitch. He chose his hand because he couldn't get pussy. I don't care anymore, though. I love you and am pleased to be with you like that.

If I returned to him, I wondered whether I would be happy and if he would keep playing with me. I didn't think or maybe want to commit again, but Phoebe, you are much better than him. You treat me better than he ever would. I treat you right or good? God, you saved my life and gave me much better than he ever would. I'm happy for you.

I fucked you last night, and I enjoyed it. When I fucked Curtis at least on a one-night stand, I would have still been up for it, but he didn't have to let me fall so much in love with him. If he knew, he was going to dump me later. I hate him, though. I found a love with you that is better than anything else.

I'll see you at our secret place, Damian.

"I just don't understand," Tony said. "It sounds like a guy who doesn't know who he is."

"At that age, did you know yourself?" I asked.

"No, but I didn't treat the girl in my life like she is second best and the only reason he's with her is that this Curtis guy is a dick," Tony said.

"Maybe in his way, he's telling her he loves her," I offered with a tinge of sympathy. "I still think my mom was crazy being with a guy who likes another guy. It is better to find someone else. From the start of the letters, she has been with him for over a year." I looked in the mirror, applying the final touches to my face, hoping it would hold up under the expected tears.

"Maybe the notes tell you what your mom was like, or more what Damian was like," Tony said. "You said your mom only had one man she loved forever and always."

"Yes, but I always thought that was my dad. So when he cheated on her, it crushed her," I told him. "We moved out, and mom gave herself three days to feel sorry for herself, gathered herself, got a lawyer, and took my father to the cleaners.

"Get dressed, and we'll go. Are you hungry?"

I shook my head and slipped into a new bra and panties. "Not really."

He left me in silence to get dressed. The familiar rituals calmed me, and I felt almost human when we walked out of the car.

Chapter Fourteen

Mourners packed the funeral home. The service didn't start for half an hour. Still, we had local notables, police, detectives, and family friends to add to the volatile mix of relatives and me. I should've been here earlier. I'd never heard all about my failings before the service got underway. But, at least after the funeral, I would only have to deal with Oliver for one more day. Then, once the lawyer reads the will, I could be on my way back to San Francisco. I glanced at Tony and realized that I might not be heading to San Francisco yet, but I'd still be away from family.

Oliver was waiting for me. Someone must have tipped him off I was here. He was ready to plaster me before I even caught my bearings.

"It's about time you decided to show up," he said, staring down his nose. "You should have been here over an hour ago to meet the family. And where's my SUV?"

I didn't even slow down, and he had to leap aside to avoid me bouncing him into the wall. "Yesterday, you told me to be less involved. But Oliver, for once in your life, show some spine and make a decision. Which is it? You've been hogging the limelight, and I'm happy to let you have it. Choke on it. I left your stupid toy in the parking lot regarding the SUV."

I watched the police talking to some people, and Oliver was in a mood...Well, when was he not? Then a police officer came up to me. It was Officer Miller. "We checked out your alibi, and you were where you said you were, and that is pissing off your step-father, who insists you're the one who killed your mother for the money."

When Officer Miller left me, Oliver came up with a chip on his shoulder. He started following me, saying something I didn't get at first. He wants to get to me. The expression on Oliver's face left no doubt I'd confused him, so he switched tactics. "I don't want him here," Oliver said, sliding back in front of me and walking backward. "He threatened one of my guests, and he has no business here while I'm burying my wife. So he goes, and you're lying because my SUV isn't in the parking lot."

"Yes, it is, Oliver. I just checked," I grumbled. When I stopped, I looked for Tony and waved him back to me. "As far as Tony is concerned, then, we're even; I don't want you here, either," I assured him. "Once again, you think you're controlling my friends and me. Disabuse yourself of that idea right now. I do as I damned well please, and no one tells one of my friends that they have to leave my mother's funeral." I stepped up into Oliver's face and forced him back a step. Inside, a quiet part of me marveled at my reaction. Charlotte called me "the bulldog" when one of my friends was threatened. Again, it illustrated how Tony defied all my expectations and fit into my life.

Thinking of Tony, I lowered my voice to avoid giving Oliver another scene. "Daniel was being an ass and deserved to be thrown out of my room," I continued without pause. "And if you don't want to be thrown into a hearse, you'd better get out of my way. If I scream while the police investigate, they will be more motivated to look into my past. I may not get my way, but I will guarantee you a three-ring circus that'll make you wish you'd never been born. As for your SUV, it's out there, but if you want it towed, or better yet, stolen, I say, 'good for the crooks', though it can't be worth much, as cheap as you are.

Remember, I gave you the keys. So you can't say I stole it." His face paled as he snarled and dithered.

Before I could see if he had a pair, Dad stepped into the hall with Karla beside him. Dad was frowning like a thunderhead, and Karla was shooting cold daggers at me with her eyes. I guess she'd hoped for a late-night meeting with Tony. She was ambitious; I had to give her that.

"Young lady, I am shocked at your behavior," Dad growled. "I don't know what you're thinking, but threatening a guest of mine is inexcusable. So is running off to have an all-night orgy with a man you just met the night before your mother's funeral." He shifted his gaze to Tony. "I shouldn't have expected any better from the likes of you. Leave. You're not wanted here." Tony didn't seem at all bothered by Dad's disapproval. Or Oliver's. He looked at me and raised an eyebrow.

I shook my head. "He stays. Whether or not I slept with him is my business, Dad. I won't tell you who you can or can't sleep with, so I'd appreciate the same courtesy. What happens in Sun Valley stays in Sun Valley, you know, unless the two of you would like to change the rules?"

Karla flushed, and her cold eyes heated with rage. "Are you upset, Karla, that you didn't have time to sleep with Tony? I mean, you had my sloppy seconds the other night."

Dad's expression didn't change. "Don't change the subject.

We're speaking about you and your unacceptable behavior."

"It's my behavior that's bad, not your wife's?" I posed.

He didn't seem surprised when I said Karla cheated. Interesting, but irrelevant.

I smiled. "But Dad, I'm just being a good little daughter and following in your footsteps. All I've ever wanted was to be like you. So, if you don't want your philandering or your wife's sleeping with people like Daniel to be brought up, leave my sex life out of this."

"I don't sleep around, and neither does Karla," he said in almost apoplectic rage.

"I have a video of Karla leaving Daniel's room. Want to see it?" I didn't shoot the video myself but watching Karla's face pale was fun. I have a video. The house has video cameras all over the place. I have the video on my cell phone to show him.

His denial about his behavior fell flat for anyone who knew him. As for Karla, who knew what she believed? A better question was, who cared?

"You've pushed me as far as I'm willing to go." He leaned in, and I had to force myself to stand my ground. "That trust fund of yours and the settlements from those men you used and dumped might keep you in a comfortable house, but I know you want more. You want to be rich. I know your mother left everything to Oliver."

"That's not true," Officer Miller said behind my father, making him turn around and pale at seeing him. "Sophia, I need to see the video."

"Right now?" I asked.

"If you can?" Officer Miller asked.

"You will not show him that video," Dad said.

"Are you saying you want to hide evidence from a police officer?" Officer Miller asked.

"I would never do that," I assured him with blatant sarcasm. "I was taught to follow the law."

I pulled out my cell and pulled it up. It showed when Karla went into his room and when she left. My dad was pissed, and I could see it, but I wasn't lying, and I'm tired of people always saying I am.

Then dad started again, "If you continue humiliating me this way, I'll cut you out of my will, too." Finally, his voice dropped to a harsh whisper as he wound down.

This wasn't the first time he'd played this card to good effect. My mom said there was a safeguard, and I would get my trust no matter what after my dad pulled this on me the last year. I felt my heart rise into my throat. He thought using his money as a threat was what would motivate me. He never seemed to get that his approval made me do what he wanted. I had to make a choice now between pursuing a relationship with a man, one that would end in disaster, and making Dad happy.

Dad's stern glare told me I didn't have the luxury of time, either. I had to make that decision right here and now. Should I follow my heart or my mind? Was there a choice? As always, he held all the cards.

Then I remembered what Tony said yesterday. The past defined us, but we could break the cycle if we accept the pain and start again. Karma or redemption? Right now, I was at the cusp of two very different futures—one with Dad's approval and one with no close family. So, I took a deep breath and made the most crucial decision of my life.

"Tell you what, Dad. You give me your will and a pair of scissors, and I will cut myself out., Dad. I never wanted your stinking money. I wanted something you couldn't give me. Come on, Tony." My voice was astonishingly level, and I wasn't shaking like a leaf.

"Seems like your daughter knows more about you guys than I thought," Officer Miller said to my dad. "I will have to talk to her about who was sleeping with who the last couple of nights."

Dad looked stunned, and Karla looked triumphant as I pushed past them and into the funeral home. Oliver looked gray, but that was natural. Now I noticed all the people staring at the confrontation. I couldn't decide if gossip and innuendo spreading like wildfire were good or bad. Then, finally, I felt someone's hand on my shoulder, and I turned around to see Kim and Mike. "Your mom would have been proud of how you told your dad off. She didn't think you had it in you. Plus, you get your trust. Next year your mom had it written in the divorce degree, so you can say he will take it away, but legally he can't take it from you. So remember that."

"I think Officer Miller needs to talk to you," I said.

"He has, and I told him everything I know, Little One," Kim said. The Little One was a nickname my mom gave me.

I went to the front row and sat down with Tony, staring straight ahead.

What had I just done? Was I right? Wrong? Stupid? All the above? I felt my breathing speed up, and the tears threatened to overwhelm me.

Tony took my hand, and I looked at him through my unshed tears. "I'm so proud of you," he whispered.

I stopped a maniacal laugh in my throat through brute force.

"I've just walked away from the only family I've ever known."

He nodded. "Just like I did. Now you don't have to fit into the mold of what they expect and demand. You can be who you want to be now."

Then Officer Miller approached me and asked who was in the house the other night and who my father's wife was sleeping with other than Daniel. I found it interesting that he believed what I was saying and not the rest of my family. My father and Oliver tried to get me to stop talking to the police. Were they stupid or desperate when they both attempted to interrupt Miller twice? I learned from Officer Miller that my father was in Sun Valley during my mom's death. So was my ex-boyfriend Daniel, who was staying with my mom and stepfather before she died. That was odd because my dad told me he came from overseas, and Daniel brought his bags to the viewing and acted like he was just getting there. I told Officer Miller all that I knew.

Now I understand why my father was upset that I talked to the police about my mom's death. When Officer Miller left, Tony asked, "Did that feel good telling on your stepmother and ex-boyfriend?"

That brought a small smile. "I already have a reputation for doing what I want despite the consequences."

"I didn't say free to do what you want, Sophia. That's not the same as being free to be who you want to be."

I pulled a tissue from my purse and wiped my eyes. "I guess I don't understand the difference yet."

"We've got years to figure that out," he said confidently. "We? Planning on being around for a while?"

"For a while," he agreed with a smile. "Did Karla want to sleep with me?"

"She was looking at you like a bitch in heat," I said.

"Glad we didn't stay there last night, then," Tony began. "I would have been trying to find a way to get into your room." I blushed, and Tony smiled at me.

Oliver sat stiffly on the bench across from me as the minister walked up to the podium to start the funeral. I noticed I hadn't seen Daniel. I worried about where he was and what he was doing when I couldn't see him.

Nothing could be done about that now. So, I ignored Oliver, paying attention to the service, though I felt his gaze on me several times.

Chapter Fifteen

I cried through the funeral, but it went as well as that kind of thing can go. So many people got up and spoke about all the good things my mother had done and blessed the surrounding people. Some of it was real, but the rest was well-meaning tripe and posturing. Unfortunately, all too many people said the right thing only so they could be seen doing it.

Near the end, I stood up and made my way to the podium, cutting off Oliver before he could walk to the microphone for the final eulogy. Instead, Oliver sat back down and glared at me.

I'd decided before the funeral not to speak. That must have surprised the minister, but he took it in stride. I suppose he'd seen it all at these sorts of things. Looking out over the crowd, I felt the rising tension. They expected something terrible to happen. I imagine that meant that word of my telling Dad off had already made the rounds.

I smiled at Oliver and then at Dad for a moment. Then I focused on the crowd as a whole. "Everyone's spoken about all the good works my mother did in her life, but I don't think they've touched on the core of who she was. So let me tell you about my mother. She was a flawed woman."

At the quick inhalation of breath, I smiled a little deeper. "Yes, flawed. As flawed as we all are. Some more flawed than others." I spared a glance at Oliver without being obvious about it. "Despite her flaws, she loved me despite my flaws. She loved me, and I still love her. Maybe that seems a little off-topic from

all the grand stories here this morning, but it's what's important to me. So, despite our failures, we could love one another in our ways. I'll miss you, Mom."

Wiping my face, I resumed my seat. Tony slid an arm around me and held me reassuringly close. At the same time, Oliver walked stiffly to the podium and made the most pompous speech, seeming to focus more on him than her. Typical.

The minister closed the service and thanked everyone for coming. That seemed to cut loose the crowd, and I again broke the rules. Kim and Mike both hugged me. I walked out with my back straight, and my head held high.

Outside, I'm sure Oliver would have done something nasty if I'd bothered to stop and try to speak to him. But I blew past him without pausing. Dad and Karla were already in the parking lot, and he stared at me for a moment before deliberately turning his back and climbing into his car. Karla's grin was predatory as she followed him. I pretended it didn't hurt as Dad turned his back on me. I hope Kim was right about my trust. Why does he hate me so much?

"Come on," Tony said, leading me to his Rover through the dispersing crowd. People avoided me as if I'd caught the plague.

"Time to go get roaring drunk."

"That sounds like a grand idea," I agreed with a sigh. "Drive on." I was glad to drive to Mountain View Cemetery for the burial when they released my mom's body. After all that had happened, I couldn't bear to see her put on the ground. I couldn't, but I will ensure that is where she wants to be. We have been to the cemetery many times, and mom always said this is the place she will rest. Perhaps that is why she insisted she would read here tomorrow morning. Maybe she knew me better than I knew myself. Then, I could start reading more letters my mom wanted me to read. Why did Oliver think my mom didn't leave me anything? Why was my dad in town? Officer Miller ran to the, and Tony's SUV rolled down the window. "Can you meet me at the station, please?" "Why? You said I had an alibi," I reminded him.

"Could you please meet me at the station? I can't force you, but it would help to find your mother's killer." Officer Miller stated.

"We will follow you," Tony said. "Does she need a lawyer?"

"No, not right now," Officer Miller said, walking away and getting into his car.

"Holy shit, what do they think I did? I would never hurt my mom," I asked.

"Do you have any idea what the will says?" Tony asked.

"No, clue. My lawyer will be there during the will reading. My mom requested it."

"Call your lawyer and tell them what is going on," Tony said. So, I grabbed my cell and called my lawyer, and after talking to him, he told me having him there from the start made it look like I was hiding something. So, he wanted me to find out what was happening and then call him. I was told to give Tony my lawyer's number if I can't call until after reading.

We went into the station, having Officer Miller follow behind us. He took us through an extensive set of doors and down a hall to, I think, his office he shared with other police officers. "Have a seat, and here is a chair for you," Officer Miller said as he walked around his desk.

Officer Miller pulled out his little notebook and then looked up at me. "I have a reason for asking these questions, so please don't get upset, but at any time you want a lawyer, let me know." "What is this about?" I asked.

"First, we need your fingerprints," Officer Miller said.

"Explain," Tony said.

"You don't look like a drug addict, so the information we are getting is not making sense to me; that is why I need the fingerprints to see if the drugs are yours or if they were planted in your room. The arsenic poison was also found in your room, and we discovered that your mom was being poisoned....

slowly, the chemo treatments hid the fact."

"Drugs were found in my room?" I asked.

"Yes, but you don't look like you're using, so it makes little sense to me," Officer Miller said.

"I used drugs when I first got out of the military. Something to dull the pain was what I was looking for. I have PTSD. I got treatment six months after that and have been clean for over five years," I said.

"That's what I thought. Everyone told me you were on drugs, but I didn't see it. These people say you are a druggie, but nothing they're saying makes sense. They say you killed your mom, but you were not here, and it would have to be someone around your mom often. I know you have been in

San Francisco planning police officers' events for the last three months, so there is no way you could come back and poison your mom and go back again. I've also been told that you didn't care about your mom. You had no clue your mom was sick, to begin with. None of it makes sense, but everyone is pointing at you as the one who killed your mom."

I was stunned by what he had just said. "Why the fingerprints?"

"We have fingerprints from the drugs and the arsenic. I want to see if your prints match first before going after the rest of your family. Since everyone is blaming you, this will show you did nothing," Officer Miller said.

"I loved my mom, and I was talking to her, but she never told me she was sick. If I had known, I would have come back to see her. My mom had a style, and if she was not feeling well, she hid the fact from everyone when she was sick. You can take my fingerprints, and you can do a drug test, too," I said. I was so done with everyone thinking I was on drugs again.

Officer Miller picked up his phone and told someone to come, and another police officer came in and told me to follow her. I got up and followed her to another room with the fingerprint machine. She had me wipe off my fingers and then had a pad and roll each finger. When I was done, they took me to the bathroom and gave me a cup to fill. Then, they brought me back to Miller and Tony after I did what they asked. "I think you should call your lawyer," Tony said.

"I will if my fingerprints match," I said.

Officer Miller was doing some research on his computer.

"Just what I thought." "What's that?" Tony asked.

"They're not her fingerprints," Officer Miller said. "Did you know if your mother left money to you that her alimony goes to you for the rest of your life, but if your mom left it to Oliver, the alimony stops, and there is just a check of five hundred thousand that will go to Oliver?"

"As I said, I have no clue what the will says. No one told me,"

I reassured everyone within hearing distance. "The one thing I know is that the will was changed a month ago. The lawyer told me that."

A police officer walked out of the room after handing a piece of paper to Officer Miller. He took one glance at it and laughed.

"Again, as I predicted, you have no drugs in your system."

I took a deep breath, and so did Tony. As far as days go, this was one of the worst. My mom loved me. Now she's still at the hospital being checked out more. As far as the others.... We weren't exactly the Brady Bunch high on the holidays, but we were family. We are family. The worst part... they think I killed my mom. I don't understand why they think I killed her?

Chapter Sixteen

Stopping on the way back to the hotel, I found a bottle of François Villard St. Joseph Blanc 1996, and Tony snagged a bottle of Patterson Irish Whiskey and a bottle of Bourbon. That beat the hell out of the crap in those stupid minibars.

When we got to our room, we saw the light blinking on the phone. "Get that, will you?" Tony asked as he set the bottles on the counter.

I dialed the desk and asked for any messages. The perky female voice that answered set my teeth on edge, but I just asked for the messages.

"No messages, ma'am. We had a package delivered to your room," she said.

"A package?" I asked, surprised. "What kind of package?"

"It looks like a box of clothes," she chirped. "A man left it for your room this morning."

"I'll be right there," I said and hung up before she could respond. "I think we need to shift hotels."

Tony shrugged. "That's fine. You get the package. I'll pack and pick you up in the lobby in ten minutes. Just check us out."

With a nod, I left him packing and walked to the office. Unfortunately, the woman looked just as disgustingly perky as she sounded.

I presented my ID and room key, and she handed me a cardboard box.

I took it and opened the lid to glance inside at the contents. It looked like my clothes and had minor personal effects. On top was an envelope with my name on it. I tore it open and scanned the brief note.

Neither you nor your friend is welcome in my home any longer. Please don't come back to my property. - Oliver

I crumpled the note. "We're going to be checking out early."

Unperturbed, the cheerful clerk nodded and processed us out. I stepped outside and went through the box while I waited for Tony. Under all the clothes was another of Daniel's vials. I gritted my teeth in rage, poured them onto the ground, and scattered them with my foot. Then I crushed the vial under my shoe—that asshole.

A minute later, Tony pulled up. I put the box of clothes in the back and climbed in. Tony handed me the shoe box with the letters, and I put it on my lap. "Where to?" he asked.

"Best Western," I said. "If I'm going to be disowned, I can at least celebrate in style. For example, having a room with a Jacuzzi tub."

He shook his head and smiled at me. Then, without another word, he drove to Best Western.

Best Western, and I had a natural history. But, if you looked at it from the proper perspective, the record was both good and bad. At least one incident had been both at the same time.

I shook my head and scattered the gathering thoughts. Tony was right. The past was the past, and I couldn't choose to undo those long-ago events, even if I'd wanted to. Considering how blissfully happy Emma was now, I wouldn't change that night one bit, even though I regretted the pain I'd helped cause that night.

Ultimately, Emma's strength and independence were worth all her pain, even if I was sometimes mystified by her taste in husbands. Still, he made her happy, and if that's what she wanted, it's what I wanted for her. I didn't have to understand. I just needed to love her. I did envy the happiness she'd made for herself, though.

A glance and a smile back at Tony reinforced how life sometimes took a left turn and tossed all our plans and expectations on their heads. Maybe I needed to reevaluate my opinion about Emma's husband since I had to re-examine everything in my life. Even knowing Tony as little as I did, he and Emma's husband seemed to have a good bit in common. They were both in good shape, but more importantly, they had similar vital self-assurance. I found the similarities a bit disturbing and just a little bit ironic.

With a laugh that drew a surprised look from Tony, I rushed into the lobby and straight up to the desk clerk.

"I need a suite with a Jacuzzi," I said, sliding my ID and credit card over.

An hour later, we were ensconced in a lovely suite and sitting naked in the Jacuzzi, sipping on our drinks. Well, he was consuming, and I was closer to gulping. I expected him to tell me to slow down, but he didn't. So, after the first glow hit me, I slowed down and watched him from beneath my eyelashes.

"Aren't you afraid I'll drink myself into a stupor?" I asked.

"I wouldn't say 'afraid,' but I am worried about it," he admitted.

"Then why aren't you stopping me?"

He smiled and shook his head. "If anyone deserves to get falling-down drunk tonight, it's you, and I won't stop you. If you do, I'll ensure you get safely to bed, so don't worry about it."

"Does that involve more gentleman-like behavior?"

"Yep," he said, sipping his drink. "I won't take advantage of you while your defenses are down."

"How about we read another note?" I asked.

"I like that idea," Tony said. "Let's order pizza too."

"On it, what do you like on your pizza? I like it loaded," I said.

"Me too."

I put down my glass and picked up my cell. After a quick search and a few clicks, we had a pizza with everything on its way. It's strange, the number of times I've seen Tony wholly naked and the number of times he has seen me the same way. Yet he has never touched me, and I begrudgingly have never touched him- beyond a kiss. So why did I feel conspicuous, even self-conscious, stepping out of the hot tub to retrieve my box of letters? I put it out of my mind and began to read.

October 10, 1999

Damian

Hey, how are your two other fuck buddies? How could you? Curtis, I can understand, but not Jess. I wish I could calm down. Just fuck, fuck, fuck, you do not know. I'd rather be a helpless nympho rather than your pathetic bitch. Even so, this shit is getting old. So how did I find out? Curtis wrote me, and we talked about it. He's not happy, either.

Maybe we should stop all this shit, and you can use your left hand or find some other bitch who is stupid enough to fall in love with you. Only you will not talk to her like you do me because she won't put up with your shit. I know Jess is saying she's pregnant. Why do you have to sleep with so many people? It will just be too inconvenient. I won't talk to you because you would have to lead me on for so long. It would hurt me way too much. Well, that's how I feel. I think that is an excellent idea. Maybe you need to be without Curtis and me until you realize what you have. Then you're going to work hard to get us back, and you will see you hurt me.

Fuck you, Phoebe

"My mom was pissed, and she had every right to be," I said.

"I would have kicked his ass," Tony said. I had to smile at his chivalry. I folded the note up and started on the next.

December 4, 1999,

Damian

Hello, my love. How are you doing? You came to me last night telling me it all was a lie. First, you didn't sleep with Jess or any of the others. Then after we slept together, you went home, and this morning, I found out it's all a lie. Why did you lie to me? Why are you thinking that I'm fucking stupid? I'd find out, anyway. God, what the hell do you take me for? I should be pissed. I figure it should only be considered a lie if I find out.

Anyhow, all that shit with Jess, you realize she hates me and will kick my ass because you lied, not me. I told the truth. I would have said it's not my place to say anything and let her wonder why I said that after you lied. You wouldn't back me up. At least tell her you lied to me or something and that you got me going. You have made me lie to so many people. I don't want people hating me because of you. I don't want people hating you because of me. So I lie for you, and do you know how many times I lied to come and see you? It would be best if you were flattered. That's your handy work and a chance to smash a lot of trusts I have with many people because I love you. I'd do anything to be with you. I had to tell my section sergeant what was happening because I could get into trouble fighting someone. You don't give a shit about that either. Now I feel better about taking her out. If she throws the first punch, she goes down fast.

I worked hard this last year to get to where I am, and I'd do anything to be with you. But, Damian, all I want to be is happy, to choose one or the other. You can't have both. If you choose me, then have it be only me. If you decide Curtis, let it only be him. Okay, I want you to be happy. I do not always want to wonder if my man is cheating on me with another guy. It makes me feel low. I can't compete with another guy for your love anymore.

Please choose me, as I still love you. Phoebe

"This guy messed with my mom," I said.

"I don't understand why she is still talking to him," Tony said. I folded that note and grabbed the next.

December 5, 1999,

Phoebe

Hey, what are you doing? Me, nothing much, just sitting here doing the usual. I will talk to Jess tomorrow. Ask me about it, and

I'll tell you how it went. I have to speak to you. It's essential. I thought

I'd write you a brief note and tell you, I love you.

Damian

That's a weird note," Tony said.

"It is," I agreed, folded it up, and grabbed the next one.

December 6, 1999

Phoebe

Hey, I didn't have time to talk to Jess tonight. I found out that she lost the baby last night, and we talked about that and the fact she wants me to help her get pregnant again. I told her we needed to wait and never got to the fact that I should have her stop the fight.

So it would help if you went home until I talked to her.

I love you,

Damian

"This Jess girl is a piece of work. I bet she wasn't even pregnant," I speculated.

"I think this Damian guy is an asshole that needed to have his ass kicked," Tony said.

There was a knock on the door, and my stomach told me who it was. I folded the letter. "Pizza!"

Chapter Seventeen

As we sat down and had a piece of pizza, Tony told me to read another note. It was great to have someone as interested as I was in the notes. I still didn't understand why she had me read them, but it was better because Tony was with me. So I ate one slice, grabbed a second, took out a note, and started reading again.

Damian,

Jess is not pregnant. I asked a couple of her friends. She wants you, and that's why she told you that. Plus, the fight is to keep you. I'm so done with this crap. It's time to grow up. I'm not going home to hide. Please fix this, or I will.

Phoebe

"See, I told you so. What a bitch," I said.

"I don't understand why all these girls want him," Tony quipped. "He's the rebel. Maybe that is it, but it doesn't make sense. He's sleeping with both guys and girls, and you think the girls would want nothing to do with him."

"When I was in high school, we had a guy that said he was gay, and all the girls wanted to be with him. So I began, "I didn't understand, but my mom said that if I think about it, I would understand that girls want to be the one that says they changed him from being gay to being straight. It's like a way to get more girls to go after him. Maybe mom knew this from this Damian guy."

"Well, read the next one," Tony said.

I finished my next slice and unfolded the following note.

December 7, 1999

Phoebe

How are you, babe? What are you doing? Me, not a lot, just sitting here in the first hour. I haven't seen you in a couple of days since the fight. I saw it on the video on Paul's cell. I can't believe you let her hit you twice before you kicked Jess's ass. I didn't know you could fight like that. How is your fist?

I called you last night, but your sister said you were out. What the hell does that mean? Are you out with David?

I love you

Damian

"Good to know where I got my fighting from. It was my mom, not my dad," I said.

"What a dick!" Tony said. "If I saw him now, I would kick his ass for what he did to your mom, read another letter. Let's see if he gets his ass kicked."

"I can't believe the fight still happened. Why did my mom let her hit her twice before fighting back?"

"That way, everyone knows Jess started the fight, not your mom. I think her section sergeant had told her about that. " Tony said.

"Being hit twice is a good way to show you didn't hit them first, but you had to hope you could stand up after it," I said.

"If your mom's section sergeant was brilliant, he told her to have someone record it, so it showed she hit first and second and then told how to take her down fast," Tony pointed out. It was not lost on me how he said it, as if he was speaking from experience. "Jess would have been expelled if they were on or off school grounds. So your mom wouldn't be in trouble with the National Guard because she didn't throw the first punch or start it. Let's see what happens next."

I folded up the note and went to the next one. This should be interesting. I always knew my mom was a badass, but seeing her worried about a guy she loved says a lot. I wonder if this is the guy my mom always said she loved above all. I took a drink and then opened the following note and began.

December 10, 1999

Phoebe

Please talk to me. I'm not seeing Jess after that fight. I'm still seeing Curtis and Curtis only. He told me he doesn't care if I'm in a relationship with you as long as I share you with him. I didn't want to share with him, so I told him no. I want you, but I don't want anyone else having you, just me. But Curtis thinks it's a good idea to share it with you. I don't know where he came up with it. Curtis just told me he has a crush on you and has for a while. I didn't even know that. So please tell him no.

I love you,

Damian

"Sharing, now that's interesting," Tony said.

"I just don't understand why she keeps letting him in her life?" I questioned.

"Don't you get it? Your mom loved him even with all his faults. She still loved him." After that, I didn't know what to say and folded this letter up and grabbed the next one.

December 15, 1999

Damian

How are you? Are you tired, maybe? Since Curtis didn't meet you last night, did you stay up late or anything, I should know.

Anyway, I just thought I'd write you a letter other than a death wish to whoever is jealous of your sleeping with. He looked happy when I gave him the letter you wrote to me. So it seems like you have an excellent chance to get what you want, just not how you want it. Curtis came to me about having sex and sharing him with you. Curtis and I stayed up all night talking. We didn't sleep together, but we are thinking about it.

Well, I'm going to do what Curtis wants, and you two can share me, and we will all be one couple or a thouple if that's an accurate word. Curtis and I will take it slow, but I promised him

I wouldn't sleep with you until I sleep with him first. Curtis said that would only be fair. Do you have a decision about all this yet?

Just me,

Phoebe

"Good for mom. I'm not sure about this Curtis guy, but she is trying to get Damian to see it from her point of view," I said.

"I see this ending badly," Tony began. "Damian doesn't want this, but he wants to have his cake and eat it too."

"Would you share a woman with another man or woman?" I asked.

"No. For one night, it could be fun, but I don't share well with the person I love.

January 12, 2000

Phoebe

I can't believe you are attending the valentine's dance with Curtis. I can't think he asked you to go? Why did you say yes when I told you I wanted to take you. Why?????

Love you more than Curtis,

Damian

"This was my mom's senior year, and she told me she didn't go to Prom, so this had to be her last dance," I said.

"Your mom didn't go to Prom?" Tony asked.

"No, she told me she had National Guard drills that weekend, and they wouldn't let her out of it."

"Probably the best thing the military did for her," Tony said.

January 15, 2000

Damian

I said yes to Curtis because you cheated on both of us with Jess, and don't tell me you didn't because we know you did. Curtis and I are so pissed at you right now. You always have to have everything your way, don't you?

Done with this shit,

Phoebe

"I think mom is starting to understand what type of dumb ass this guy is," I said.

"I think your mom wants Damian and is willing to sleep with Curtis to have him in her life," Tony said. After he said that, I started thinking he might be correct. My mom seems to want Damian. She can't see that he's not a good guy. So I pulled out another letter. These are shorter but have more insight than the longer letters did. Tony has more of an idea of how my mom felt than I did. So I opened the next note and began.

January 21, 2000

Phoebe

Hello, how are you? I didn't sleep with Jess. We fooled around, that is all. Since you are not having sex with me, I need to get it somewhere else. I guess I'm just sitting here in class worrying about you. Why did you want to break my heart? It seems as if you're trying. You don't love me, and you don't care for me. I feel hated. These words hurt, and yes, I did sleep with Jess and her friend. Curtis is not worth it. Phoebe, you're better than that. He fucks with your head to make himself feel better. He doesn't think about anybody but himself. I'm not trying to turn you against him because I know I can. I'm not scheming here or anything like that because it's pointless. I understand your feelings for him; you can't be with me. You're my best friend and the best fuck I've been with. I love every cubic inch of you and your heart and soul because I know who you are.

I love you, Damian

"He's a piece of shit," I said.

"He's using her to get what he wants, and right now, Damian is seeing how much pull he has on your mother," Tony said.

Chapter Eighteen

January 24, 2000

Phoebe

Why are you so upset with me? Curtis isn't even talking to me now. How did you get him on your side? I miss you both, and I slept with Jess, and Marie has nothing to do with it. You can tell Jill to stick it. This is none of her business. Why is she being such a bitch to me? She told me I shouldn't be sleeping around, and I told her that we agreed that I could. So will you tell her?

I love you,

Damian

Based on what I've read, they agreed to sleep with other people but not someone out of the three. "That's weird. Did I miss a note that said they could sleep around?" I asked.

"Nope, I didn't see any note that said he could sleep around," Tony said. I think this guy is a piece of work, and I found out he was in prison is enough said. So I took out the next batch of notes and opened the next one.

Damian

We had an agreement to sleep with each other, not someone else! So what the hell are you thinking about. Jill has a right to tell me. You're being a dick because you are. I haven't slept with Curtis, but that all changes tonight. Curtis wants us to break up with you, and I told him I would do it. So we are breaking up with you.

Please don't write or call me, and Curtis is adding his request to this note. Phoebe

Damian

I can't believe you lied to Jill like that. We agreed that we only sleep with each other, and that is all. I decided I wasn't sleeping with you until I slept with Phoebe because you told her not to sleep with me. As always, you lied and told everyone what you wanted. I'm done. Phoebe is my everything, and I'm keeping her. I'm sleeping with Phoebe after or during the dance. You can stick it, and we are broken up! Phoebe is mine and mine only now.

I love Phoebe and not you,

Curtis

That shocked me, and they finally had enough of Damian. "Well, do you think mom stayed away?" I asked.

"I don't think so; there are more notes here," Tony began. "Wow, this guy is messed up. He wanted them to agree with him even when he was wrong." I folded the note. I was done for the night.

I set my wineglass on the side of the tub and slid over to him in hot water. Surprised, he barely had time to develop his drink before I sat in his lap and pulled his arms around my waist. I ran my hands across his chest, feeling the stiff muscles under his soft skin.

"Well, my defenses aren't down right now, or at least they're up as far as they need to be. So, what if I want you to take advantage of me?" I nipped his earlobe gently. "What if I want you to make love to me right now? I don't understand why I feel so close to you, much less so quickly, but I don't want to fight it anymore. Do you want me, Tony?"

A slow smile spread on his face as I felt him rise to the occasion until he was firm against my thigh. I moved and allowed him to unbend himself. Then I rubbed myself against his erection. His eyes lost focus, and he pulled me against him and kissed me deeply.

I melted into him as the emotions I'd held in check suddenly rushed through my mind. This was like making love to Emma or Charlotte, but somehow not quite the same. I kissed him back with an ardor that surprised me. I was suddenly hungry for him in the worst way.

The world shrunk to the two of us as his hands found my breasts. The sweet mixture of pleasure and pain when he bit my nipples made me gasp. I felt so hot inside that the hot tub felt cool.

He stopped me when I reached down to guide him inside me. "No, let me make love to you."

Surprised and confused, I nodded and stood up uncertainly. He pulled me out of the tub and dried me thoroughly. The soft caress of the towel drove me crazy, and he seemed to know where to touch me.

He dried quickly, led me slowly into the bedroom by the hand, and sat me on the edge of the bed. I watched him curiously to see what he had in mind.

Taking my face in his hands, he kissed me slowly and deeply. I felt that kiss down to my toes. Then he let his lips travel all over my face and neck, kissing and gently nipping my skin. Gasps and moans escaped my lips as he continued his slow torture.

His hands cupped my breasts. He licked and nipped my neck, his hands gently squeezing and twisting my nipples in evergrowing sharp twists. He quickly discovered that I liked my nipples mistreated.

My eyes watched him lustfully, and I tried pulling his head back to kiss me. But, unfortunately, that got his hands to capture my wrists and hold them pinned at my sides.

"Oh, no," he whispered hungrily. "I'm going to kiss every inch of your body before we make love. No shortcuts." That fired a jolt of pure lust through my body. I was instantly drenched inside. When he let go of my hands, I forced them to remain at my sides as he resumed his slow progress.

I was breathing heavily by the time his mouth captured my right nipple. I sucked in my breath, and my back arched convulsively. He licked, bit, and sucked it until my hips were thrusting rhythmically. I moaned at every gentle nip of his teeth. I don't remember tangling my fingers in his hair, but he didn't complain this time. The sensations had far surpassed anything I'd ever felt with a man before, and I began to think I would come just from his lips on my breasts.

Groaning, I again tried to fight him for control. I wanted him inside me, and I wanted it now!

He quickly pinned me back on the bed. "No, no, no," he grinned. "That gets you two minutes in the penalty box."

"God," I groaned in frustration. "How can you stand this? Fuck me, Tony. Please, fuck me!"

"Good things come to those who wait," he teased. "Patience is a virtue."

I almost screamed, but he only laughed and kissed my inner arm, working slowly toward my wrist. With my arms trapped in his hands, I couldn't even touch myself. I writhed, attempting to rub against him for relief. But, again, Tony laughed and didn't cooperate.

By the time he worked his way down my stomach, I was sure I would die. It felt like I'd been on the brink of a massive orgasm for hours. Every minute was the most exquisite torture. As he kissed my inner thigh, I felt the moisture of my arousal run down my ass. I could only imagine the massive wet spot.

Then he started away from my sex and down toward my knee, and I did scream. "Oh, God!"

Tony laughed and kept kissing, licking, and nibbling me slowly. Then, finally, he made me bend my knee and kiss down to my feet, licking and sucking the arch of my foot. It was so close to tickling that I almost kicked him, but it was also erotic in a way I'd never imagined. Then, when he sucked my toes and gave each one a petite blowjob, I felt it up to my spine, and my eyes closed in pleasure.

He repeated that fantastic performance on my other foot and started back up my other leg. I knew what was coming now, and I was so ready that I just knew I was going to cream all over him at the first touch of his lips on my sex. Inch by a torturous inch, he covered the distance, seeming to slow down as he came closer to his goal. When his nose touched my pubic hair, my hips thrust uncontrollably, and I urged him on with soft groans and moans.

He settled between my legs and blew softly on my pussy.

Finally, he pushed me to the very brink of orgasm without having touched my sex even once. As he leaned forward, I tensed in anticipation, the moment drawing out almost painfully. Then, all of a sudden, he rolled me onto my stomach. "Time for the back half," he said in that infuriatingly cheerful voice.

I lost it. I completely lost my marbles right there. I begged. I pleaded. I threatened. I insulted. All that got me was more time in the penalty box. Then, remorselessly, he started at my neck and worked his way down my back. Goosebumps covered every inch of me, and I felt like floating.

His teeth on my ass while his hands squeezed my butt cheeks made me start grinding into the bed. He had to pull one hand back to pull me away from the promise of gratification. That precipitated a war for control of my hands again, which I quickly lost.

"You're almost there," he encouraged me, his warm breath flowing along the crack of my ass. "Just a few minutes more..." Then he gently spread the globes of my ass and ran his tongue along my rosebud. Lightning flashed through my brain as he gave me the rimjob of my life. I'd usually been the giver of anal pleasure, and now he was driving me crazy.

I was almost too incoherent to feel when he flipped me back over and onto my back. Then he buried his face between my legs and split me with his tongue while two fingers plunged inside me. I thought the world had ended. I don't know how long he had kept me on the brink of orgasm, but that pushed me over like a barrel over Niagara Falls. After that, I was unstoppable, and he tortured me in a frenzy of licks, sucks, and plunging fingers. One after another, the orgasms rolled over me and through me like an electric current as I writhed under his glorious torment.

Chapter Nineteen

Groggily, I focused on Tony's grinning face, which seemed to float over me. I blinked and stretched languorously. Then, "Dear God," I whispered. "What did you do to me?"

"I like to call that 'around the world in eighty minutes,'" he said, kissing me softly. His face was thoroughly drenched with my juices.

"If I had any energy left, I'd hit you for torturing me like that, you bastard," I said with a sigh.

"You'd better have some energy," he smirked, "because the main event is about to begin."

I grabbed him by the hair and pulled him on top of me, luxuriating in the feel of his body against mine. Then, I rolled him onto his back and broke our kiss. "After you call all the shots, I need a little cowgirl action. So lie back like a good boy, and let me go with you."

With a laugh, he surrendered and put his hands behind his head. "I'm yours. Do your worst."

Hungrily eyeing his cock, I decided I wanted a little taste of him first. Just enough to get him all wired to go crazy when I was ready to fuck him silly. I could get some more of that talented tongue of his. I wasn't prepared to say he ate pussy better than Emma, but he certainly knew his way around one.

With a quick twist, I slid on top of him and ground my pussy in his surprised face while I used my hand slowly to jack his cock. "Get back to licking me while I warm up the quarterback." My

eyes grew heavy-lidded as he wrapped his arms around my ass and dove in tongue first. Oh, yeah, this man would go far.

Licking my lips, I lowered my face to his cock and took the head of it into my mouth. His masculine taste exploded across my tongue, and I gloried in the velvety warmth of his cock. I wrapped my lips around him and felt his pulse in the most intimate way imaginable. His heartbeat thundered inside my mouth.

When he started thrusting his hips, I used my hands to foil him from fucking my mouth. This was payback. I was going to torture him and then fuck him after he lost his mind. Slowly, I built my tempo until I took half his length at each plunge at the same thrust he was trying to use on me. As his oral technique suffered, I knew I was affecting him.

As his precum became abundant, I pulled him out of my mouth and began jacking him off. Every few jerks, I'd lick his head thoroughly. This was when I discovered that instead of being the expected chore, going down on him excited me far more than men had in the past. Even the taste of his precum was exciting.

Taking a deep breath, I changed my plans and plunged my mouth down on his cock, inhaling and trying to suck him deep into my throat. I wanted to caress him with my throat muscles.

Unfortunately, I'd never been fond of giving head, so I choked a little and backed off to use my lips and tongue. Maybe Emma could give me some pointers...?

Tony must have liked it, though. I thought he would throw me off with the thrusting, which made me very pleased with myself. So I started sucking him as if I meant it. Usually, having a man come in my mouth was a gift to him, but I greedily wanted to treat myself this time.

I barely had a moment's warning when he arched wildly, and his cock began swelling in my mouth. I pulled back until only the head was in my mouth and used my hands to stroke his length as he came. Then, as his cum exploded across my tongue,

I rejoiced. At this moment, I wanted his to go in my mouth more than I'd ever wanted anything before. One swallow and then another, and he trailed off into mild twitches and moans. But I wasn't done with him yet. It was payback for earlier. Even as he collapsed, I licked him clean and spun over him again. Before he knew it, he was deep inside me, and I arched my back and groaned at the ceiling. My strap-on wasn't even in his league. It was good, but a real man was much, much better. I hadn't been with a man since my last divorce, and I'd almost given up on anything but women, but now, I felt more alive than I had in years.

Leaning forward, I let my hair cover his chest. Then I started grinding myself against him, bouncing slowly. I could tell it was a rough transition for him. He was probably sensitive, and here I was, forcing him to ride out that feeling. What a bitch, I thought with a grin. I was impressed that he didn't complain.

For a while, we ground together, and I started having a string of petite orgasms while I fucked him. That urged me on to a faster pace, and soon I was bouncing up and down so hard that I would've been afraid the bed would collapse if I'd had the attention to spare.

At what I thought was the height of those orgasms, Tony rolled me over and began thrusting himself deeper into me. Then I discovered I only thought I knew how intense it could get.

I clung to him, unable to do anything but scream and writhe with my sex jerking up to meet his fevered thrusts. My mouth locked to his, and I tried to suck his tongue down my throat while he built to a crescendo on top of me. Finally, my entire body spasmed, and I locked my legs around his waist, moaning his name into his ear while I held him.

He pinned me to the bed with an intense thrust. I felt him swell inside me, and then his cock convulsed as the hot, wet sensation of his come filled me. I squeezed him repeatedly with my internal muscles, milking him with the velvet glove of my pussy.

A hot, sweaty tangle of limbs, we collapsed together and whispered to each other. It didn't take long to get that this was more than hot sex. I loved him. That emotional connection to him was there in a way I could never have dreamed of with a man. I loved him. I'd thought I'd thrown my life away, but I'd only found it.

I finally realized that he was telling me something repeatedly. "I love you." I knew men used it to get what they wanted from women, but this time I somehow knew deep inside that it was real.

"I think I love you, too," I whispered dreamily back, shocking myself. My mouth seemed to have developed a mind of its own.

What the hell was I saying?

I lay there thinking about it as he drifted to sleep beside me. I finally trusted my instincts and let sleep drag me into the most beautiful dreams.

Chapter Twenty

We made slow and gentle love in the morning sunlight when we woke the next day. It was so unlike what I associated with sex. It was a slow, sensual, ever-deepening closeness, not a mad rush of pleasure. Of course, the orgasms were there for me, but the genuine treasure was the developing feelings between the man making love to me and me.

Afterward, lying in his arms, I felt more at peace with myself than I thought. I didn't want the moment to end. I wanted to lie with him forever, but that wasn't in the cards. I sighed and nestled closer to Tony, shielded and safe in his arms.

"I don't want to go," I said, "But I need to. I need to finish this."

He kissed my nose and pulled my head to his chest. "I'll go with you. I'll stuff him in a trash compactor if Oliver starts something."

I laughed. "You'd ruin the trash."

Reluctantly, I got out of bed. We showered together, and a little fooling around almost got us sidetracked.

As we dressed, I watched Tony, admiring his body. But then, he just grinned at me.

"What do we do now?" I asked, a little afraid of the possibilities. "Can you go to LA, or will that ruin your work?"

"I have an excellent relationship with the company, so I can take a leave of absence to go to LA. So we'll figure it out there,"

he said. "There's no need to rush. Let's take this one step at a time and do this right."

Grateful, I let out a breath I didn't realize I was holding. "That makes me feel better." I gave him a soft kiss. "Thank you."

He grinned and swatted my ass. "Get dressed, and let's go. Finish this so we can start the rest of our lives." I felt dizzy at the implication of his words. With a smile, I dressed and had a text telling me the meeting for the reading was pushed back for three hours because of my stepfather.

We had a knock on the door, and Officer Miller was there. "Hello, we were told you had drugs with you, and since your father is forcing this, we need to check."

"This is getting crazy. You know Sophie is not doing drugs. Do you need to test me next?" Tony said.

"That won't be necessary; all I need Sophie to do is to file a complaint against her stepfather and father," Officer Miller said. "I need to check your room and your car. While doing that, Sophie, please file that complaint so I can stop bugging you."

I think Officer Miller was grateful to give me the phone number as I was to get it. I started dialing as his boys began their methodical search for imaginary blows. Finally, I made the call and made the complaint. Apparently, if an asshole calls the cops to make a false claim enough times, it can come back to bite them in the ass. I didn't know that, but my father and step-father had hit their limit. Officer Miller didn't look happy he was here again. When I filed the complaint, I looked out to see Tony open his vehicle and then stare with his arm folded as Officer Miller and another officer clambered through it. I can only hope Tony has the patients of Jobe.

I walked out to them and asked, "How did you know we were here?"

"Your father called all the hotels and motels trying to find you after they called last night, and we told them you were no longer at the hotel you were at before," Officer Miller said. "Yes, it is against the law to have the staff tell them you were here." "So, who do I have to yell at?" I asked.

"No one. I've already filed tickets on your behalf," Officer Miller said. "All clean, just as I thought. Was there anything planted on you?"

"Yes, my stepfather brought me a box with some drugs; we threw them away," I said.

"Good to know; see you at the lawyer's office in a couple of hours," Officer Miller said as he squeezed into his car.

"Do you know who killed my mom yet?" I asked.

"We are getting close. We know your mother knew she was being poisoned. She left a video and a letter with her assistant. Your step-father fired her on the day you came back," my new cop friend said. "We have to wait for the reading of the will, and then we will hopefully have all this make sense. See you soon." He drove away, leaving us confused.

"Let's go get breakfast. We can read more notes," Tony said.

I was trying to get myself to relax some.

So I grabbed the last four notes and one envelope left in the shoe box. I saw pictures at the bottom, but I decided to go through them after getting back. For now, it was time for the complimentary breakfast at the motel.

We at down to a steaming plate of traditional breakfast favorites with a tall glass of orange juice. It was the coffee I had first and last. I got a few drops.

June 6, 2000

Damian

Hello, How are you? Me, I'm alright. I guess on my way to Columbia, South Carolina. That was a beautiful ring you bought for Curtis and Jill. I like her that much, after sleeping with me last night. But unless you're doing it to make Curtis jealous, I doubt it is working. I cried today, Damian, and just like last time, I'll say I will not cry over that fool anymore. Then I sleep with you, and I'm a mess again. Why do we yearn for those we cannot have? Yet why do we hurt them? They hurt themselves. I have no hope left at all, Damian.

Only wish and dream, and all will just be gone, but of all the memories, I can't believe I slept with you last night, and you gave a ring to Jill and then Curtis after. I wanted to press the rewind button the previous night. Curtis said he never agreed with Jill and you together, so that is at least something in my favor. So life goes on right. You and Jill make one hell of a messed-up couple. But if she makes you happy, I will let it go. I'm going to be happy for myself.

Without you, I will be satisfied.

Damian, I'm saying goodbye.

Phoebe

"Why did she sleep with him again? I thought she was over him?" I asked the universe.

"Sounds like they were drinking. I've made many mistakes while under the influence of the juice," Tony smirked.

"Do you have any babies or ex-wives I should know about since you know my past?" I said.

"I have one ex-wife; she was a piece of work. Your mother helped me find a lawyer and helped me with the divorce. After that, I worked for your mom doing many projects at her house," Tony said.

"I knew you had worked for my mom; I didn't know she helped you out of the divorce," I said. "How long have you known my mom?"

"Most of my life, to be honest. I told you my dad was friends with your mom when we first met."

"You told me that. How did my mom help you?" I asked.

"Mex got me to marry her by telling me she was pregnant. Then, when we got married, she lost the baby. After two years of no child, and trust me, I wanted one; after that, I found out she had been taking birth control pills the whole time. When I questioned her, she said we were not making enough money to have a child."

"What did you do next?"

"So I worked more hours to make more money, but we didn't have any saved, and that was because she was buying clothes and having her hair and nails done weekly. I never wanted to be that guy who watched how much money my wife was spending, so I told her I was making less and putting the rest into savings."

"Did it work?"

"At first, it did," Tony grumbled. "Six months later, I found out she was cheating on me. I got drunk one night and ended up at your mother's house. She always told me if I needed help to come and see her. So the drunk me remembered and went to her house. I woke up the next day in a bed, and when I came down, I couldn't remember anything that had happened that night. Your mom called her lawyer, and I was divorced in two months. It's a long story, but the short of it is, I didn't know at first that your mom called in a private detective to follow my wife around and then gave all the proof to the lawyer, and the papers were signed. I didn't have to give her anything other than what was hers. She didn't take my business, and I sold the house and gave her half. I was just glad to be done with her. After that, when I'm in town, I see your mom. I was told I couldn't see her because of cancer, but I sent texts telling her she was strong and could make it. Would you like to see them?"

"Yes, please." Tony handed over his cell. There were texts about feeling better and that she wanted him to remember her the way she looked before cancer and if he could help Sophie if she needed it.

"That's how you knew who I was the first time we met?" I said.

"Yes. Your mother's assistant texted me telling me you would need help," Tony said.

"Ms. Johnson texted you," I began. "I wonder if she's the one who put the shoebox of notes on my bed?"

"I was thinking the same thing." Tony mussed.

I grabbed my cell and texted Ms. Johnson. I've only known her all my life. I never knew her first name, but she watched me with her two kids as a child. She left it for me. I received a text back from her. She said yes when I asked if she wanted to keep her job. I told her it was hers. I didn't care; I had money, and she could care for me like my mom. I texted her to call Officer Miller and tell him anything else she knew about my mom's death, even if it sounded dumb. She told me she would call the office immediately. After reading the will, I told her we would talk about the working stuff.

"I wonder if she knows anything about the will?" I said out loud to myself.

Chapter Twenty-One

"I know your mom and Ms. Johnson were close," Tony said.

"Ms. Johnson has been with us since my mom divorced my dad. So if anyone knows what is in the will, Ms. Johnson knows. I don't care what is in the will. There are things I want, but they're not worth much. So Oliver is correct. I have money, and if I use it, I can live off it for the rest of my life. I haven't gotten money from my dad in years. I got the money from the trust I get next year, but that's gone now, and my mom always puts money into my account even when I tell her she doesn't have to. She tells me it's my money. I never understood her telling me that. My mom has enough money to live five lifetimes and still has plenty to spare. I want to have the house because that's where I was raised."

"Let's read the next letter," Tony suggested.

June 7, 2000

Phoebe

How is AIT? It's hard without you, but I understand wanting to join the Army so you can attend school. Damien gave me an engagement ring today, and I found out that Damian gave one to Jill to piss you off and make you stay here. So I gave the callback. Damian put something in your drink at the party so you would sleep with him. I found this out from Mike, who told me Damian was talking about how he got you into bed again. I know you slept with him, but I understand why you did. So I'm going to wait for you, my love. I want to marry you and have Damian out of our lives.

Love you,

Curtis

"Wow, Damian slipped her something to get her to sleep with him." Tony was shocked by what we had just read.

"This guy needs to die," I said. I was folding the note up and grabbing the next.

June 20, 2000,

Phoebe

Hey, my friend. There are things you need to know. I was sitting here in summer school in speech and writing you a letter instead of writing a speech about my greatest fear. I cried last night. Whenever I think I'm over you, someone talks about you, which fucks things up again. Jill is pregnant, and her parents came to my house and demanded I marry Jill. I know you didn't think I was sleeping with her, too. I was supposed to write my speech, but my greatest fear happened. Curtis died last night in a car crash. There was a party, and the drunk driver hit another car. It's all over the news today, but they're not giving out the name of the information yet. I know you wanted nothing to do with me, but I think Curtis will want us to be together. Would you please call or write to me? I need to tell you how much I love you. I want you back.

Love,

Damian

Neither of us said anything at first. "I can't believe he told her that way," I said. My poor mom looked like she loved Curtis, and the dumb-ass who played mind games was still playing mind games with her. What about Jill? She is pregnant; was it his plan to dump her for my mom.

"That guy knows how to play mind games. So glad he's in prison now," Tony said.

"This is the last note," I told him. "My voice was solemn when I said it, then there is an envelope left," I said.

"Well, let's hear it, and then you can open the envelope alone if you want," Tony said. Being given a choice is something I don't get very often.

August 1, 2000

Phoebe

After our phone call last night, you didn't give me time to think, and I said something I shouldn't have. When I said you should kill the baby, I didn't mean it. I know it could be Curtis's or mine. Are you marrying the man you met while you were at AIT? I don't understand why. You could come back, and I could match you instead of Jill, and then when you're at work, I can watch our baby. That sounds better than marrying Jill. I know you and Jill were friends most of your life. I don't understand how you can leave me for a guy you don't know much. You told me he cared for you and the baby, but the baby is Curtis's or mine. And yes, I said you should have killed it, but I was high last night and unsure what I was saying. If you don't come home and be with me, I will kill myself, and it will be your fault. If the baby is Curtis's child, I should raise it, not just you. Think about what I just said.

You told me last night that the guy can't have kids of his own but has to have one to get his inheritance. Marrying him would set you up for life, but I don't think it is correct. The guy is using you to get rich, and you're letting him. You told me it was his idea, but I wouldn't say I liked it. You're mine, and he can't have my baby or you.

Love you always,

Damian

"I was born in February 2001. So who is my father?" Knowing now that the man I called Dad is not my dad and how he treats me makes sense.

"Well, I don't think it's the man you've been calling father all these years," Tony said.

"Your right. He is not, but I love him."

Chapter Twenty-Two

The offices of Loveless and Loveless looked suitably posh for Mother to retain. With her, appearances meant everything, and this place screamed money and influence. Creamy marble and expensive wood dominated the hard surfaces, and overstuffed leather furniture graced the wide-open space.

The receptionist, a young woman in a designer blouse and sweater, gave Tony a discreet once-over and smiled at us. Then, when I identified myself, she showed us to a conference room.

I sat and twirled slowly in one of the executive chairs, feeling my uncertainty creep back on me. Why the hell was I even here? Oliver was going to make a sweep of Mother's possessions and gloat. Part of me still regretted losing that much money, but I grew more used to the idea; it didn't hurt quite the same way now. Honestly, I was more irked that Oliver would get his way than anything else.

Ms. Johnson came in ten minutes later, and I got up and gave her a big hug. Ms. Johnson always felt like my second mom.

Her kids didn't like me much, but I was okay with that. I'm a girl; they were both boys and were always getting into trouble. She had blond hair and blue eyes; I knew mom was protective of her, but I didn't know why. You don't think of things as a kid, and then when you're an adult, you start to wonder. So I didn't understand why this woman, who had been in my life and my mother's, wasn't at the funeral, so I asked her.

"Why weren't you at the funeral?"

"Oliver said if I came to the funeral, he would have me arrested for stealing," Ms. Johnson said, crying. "He's an evil man, and I took nothing. So if it was anyone, it was Daniel." "How long was he there before mom died?" I asked.

"Two months, your mom told him to leave many times, but Oliver wouldn't have it," Ms. Johnson said. "You want me to come and work for you?"

"Yes," I told her. "You're my second mom, and I will need you to help me through all this crap going on," I said.

"Tony!" Ms. Johnson hugged him. "I've missed you. Why are you here?"

"To make sure Sophie doesn't kill Oliver, but I might just do it for her," Tony said.

The door opened, and Officer Miller came in. "I'm not late, am I?"

"Nope, you're not late," I said.

Right on the stroke of ten, the door opened, and an older man in a tailored suit walked in with a large folder in his hand. He had that distinguished look that control and power brought to a man, and he used it well to hold himself apart from us even as he shook our hands.

"Good morning. My name is Michael Loveless, and I'll handle the reading and execution of Mrs. Masterson's will."

I grimaced as he said that. Having Mother even attached to Oliver's name irked me.

As Mr. Loveless sat down, he opened the folder, revealing papers and three DVDs. "Miss Thomas, Ms. Jill Johnson, and Mister Masterson, please allow me to express my condolences for your loss." He stopped when I held up my hand.

"I'm sorry, but there's been a misunderstanding," I said. "I'm

Miss Thomas. This is Ms. Johnson, but this isn't Mister Masterson. This is my friend Tony Di Ricco. He's here for moral support."

The lawyer apologized for the mistake and closed the folder. "I hope you'll understand, but we must wait for Mister Masterson since all three of you must be present to read the will."

"My mother left a video for us?" I asked, hearing the tremor in my voice. I'd expected the dry reading of what went where and perhaps some words from on high about how I should do better in the future. But how would those words change if she only could see me now?

The lawyer nodded. "I can't go into the specifics just yet, but she left a personal message to be played to both of you."

Tony held my hand under the table, and we waited, and waited, and waited some more. To where Mister Loveless excused himself and made some calls. The receptionist got us some coffee while we all spoke quietly as we waited. I wanted to read the last envelope, so I pulled it out of my purse. Then I had many questions and needed to know if this was the Jill in the letters.

"Ms. Johnson, did you marry Damien?" I asked.

"Sophie, you can call me Jill, and yes, I did right out of high school," Jill said.

I grabbed the letter out of my purse and looked at it. I twirled it in my fingers, glancing at the front, then back, then front again, over and over. Do I want to open it now or later? I thought. So I opened it now. We waited almost forty-five minutes, and Oliver was still not there. So I tore the last letter open and found a computer disk and a letter, and I started reading to myself.

My Dear Little One,

I know you are hurting right now and need support. That's why in the will I have Ms. Johnson looking after you. So call it getting one last gift from me. Ms. Johnson has always been like a mother to you.

As for me not telling you I was sick, I planned to have you come home right after I found out. But unfortunately, I discovered I had been being poisoned for a long time, and my doctor told me there wasn't much he could do for me. I don't know if I would have survived cancer because the poisoning was killing me faster. But I knew I had little time, so I started recording things around my house to find out who was doing it. I think I did.

I stopped reading and looked at the disk before handing it over to Officer Miller. I started reading the letter, but this time aloud, beginning from the part she was being poisoned. Now everyone in the room could hear what my mom had to say. Now she could be heard.

"*... not telling you I was sick. Right after I found out, I planned to have you come home. But unfortunately, I discovered I had been poisoned for a long time, and my doctor told me there wasn't much he could do for me. I don't know if I would have survived cancer because the poisoning was killing me faster. I knew I had little time, so I started recording things around my house to find out who was doing it. I think I did.*

The disk has video proof of what was happening and who killed me. Watch it and then give it to the police department because everyone will think I died from cancer, but it wasn't cancer. When I found out about the poisoning, there was nothing I could do, Little One, so don't think I didn't want to see you at the end. I did more than anything, but I was afraid the family would blame you because Oliver was such a sweet talker and liar. Please stay away from Daniel. He is a very evil man. I wish I could have introduced you to Tony. I think you would have gotten along with him well.

Ms. Johnson has all the paperwork, which I will talk about right now. My divorce degree has some things you need to know about. First, after reading all the letters, you know, I married your father because he was in a bind and I thought it would fix both our problems. The thing is, I had something put into the prenup that protected both of us. Second the trust: your father can't take it away because it was part of the divorce package. He can repeatedly say it's not yours but will be yours when you turn thirty next year. As for the spousal support, when I die, it is transferred to you until your death. Again, this was in the prenup, so don't let your father say this is false. As for your father, he is not your biological father, but he tried until I caught him cheating. Then everything fell apart. Everything I did was to protect you because you were my heart and still are. As for Damien and Curtis, I had a DNA test done on Damien after my divorce, while Ms. Johnson got hers. The envelope is sealed. I have not opened it. I didn't want to know. See, I loved Curtis so much and hated Damian. In the end, I didn't want you to feel that hate. I like to think you're Curtis's child, and I see him in you, but I also see Damian.

Your father never poisoned me. He was here the whole time with me, and we were getting close again. However, your father is hurting and wants to marry me again. That's what he said. He talked about our trips and promised never to cheat if I married him again. Your dad learned I was the best thing in his life, and now that I'm leaving, it hurt him more. Your father is planning on divorcing, which has much to do with Daniel and Oliver's project. So when you see your stepmom slap her in the face for me, you know why.

I have been helping some family members out of some cash problems. So now it's up to you whether you want to help them. I know they have not been friendly to you, but I think that will change when they find out who is controlling the money, or you can let them all go because of how they have treated you. I warned them they needed to be nicer to you, but they didn't do it knowing them.

So have fun with that.

Oliver has told your dad and me you are on drugs again, but I didn't think you were, but I put in steps in the will if you are because I love you so much. I don't think you are, but your father is upset about it. You know your father, when someone says something, he believes it until it is proven wrong. Promise to hug your dad every day you are around him. He is going to need it.

One more thing, I know you believe your father doesn't love you. That is so far from the truth. He doesn't know how to react around you. Remember that when you are around him.

Love you always, Little One,

Mom"

Chapter Twenty-Three

When my dad entered the room, I tried to stop crying by handing the letter to Officer Miller. He had no choice but to hug me back after I ran up to him. "I love you, Dad," was all I said, and he hugged back just as hard. Officer Miller left the room with the disk and the letter. He promised I'd get it back after the trial.

At almost eleven, Oliver strolled in with the frowning lawyer behind him. Oliver seemed unnaturally cheerful and didn't acknowledge us in any way, not even to protest Tony being there. That was so out of character that it set off my asshole warning system. I didn't know what his game was, but something was happening. His perfunctory apology satisfied no one and was just another reason to dislike him. Finally, when he saw my Dad, he stopped acting like the asshole he was and just sat down.

The lawyer opened the folder, pulled out one of the DVDs, and slid it into the player below the recessed television at the end of the room. "Mrs. Masterson left her final will verbally on this recording. The staff of this firm witnessed it. Her written will also specify the same wishes. She didn't have to make the recording," he assured us, "but insisted on doing so. It was made less than a month ago, right here in this room."

When the picture came on, Mother was sitting in a chair in front of the same paneling I could see to my left. She looked like... Mother: proud, assertive, and supremely self-confident. The fact that she wore the same dress she was buried in was enough to creep me out completely. Tony noticed and slipped his arm around me, and my father took my hand.

God, she was so young! The pain of losing her hit me all over again. She was only in her sixties. She should've had decades of life left. It was so unfair.

"I'm dead," my mother said on the TV. "I know I have breast cancer, and it will kill me, probably within a few months." If that news bothered her, she didn't choose to share the emotion with us.

"I could've let everyone know, but I didn't want to start a three-ring circus in my ultimate days. I wanted to die in peace. Hopefully, I did so." She smiled a small smile. "You know me, though; I just couldn't resist controlling the chaos I'm leaving behind."

That was the truth. I snorted, which earned a sharp look from Oliver.

"My will is short and sweet," she continued. "Jill, my best friend who has stood by my side for as long as I can remember, as we had discussed, I want you to work for Sophia, she will miss me when I'm gone, and you have always been there for Sophia and myself. So be blunt and tell her what you think, just like you did with me. Now I left you a million dollars to continue working for my daughter until you decide you don't want to work with each other anymore. I was going to give you the money and say do something fun, but you told me what you wanted, and that was to watch over our girl." I knew Ms. Johnson raised a couple of her grandkids because her son and the kids' mother were in prison. Mom let the girl come over when they were not in school, and I had even fed them when they were babies.

"As for Sophia." I sat straighter and then smirked at myself I still jumped at her call. "I know we've had our disagreements over the years. I'm not the least bit sorry for that." She nodded her head forward. "I am sorry that we weren't closer than we were. Despite my disapproval of your lifestyle, I want you to know that I love you, and I'm sorry that we never had the chance to grow closer. That is the one regret I have and the one way I've failed you."

Tears filled my eyes. The lawyer had to stop the video while I regained my composure. She could have called me any time to ask me to come, and we could have talked. Or maybe we couldn't have. Perhaps it had been too late. Perhaps we were so alike that it had always been too late.

When I could continue, the lawyer started the video again, and Mother continued. "That said, I hope one day you will get your life under control and find someone that makes you happy. A man. Sophia, you need a good man in your life." But she conveyed her subtle disapproval of all my bisexual antics with one word—another thing she never understood about me. I looked over at Tony, and he kissed my cheek. Dad saw it and said nothing.

"William, I asked you to be here because you need to support your daughter, and I hope you are. I wish I could have been there when Karla was served her paper. I hope I get to watch it wherever I'm, and I'll be laughing. Wil, I love you very much. I would have liked to return to South Carolina and redo our first date again. So, the answer to the question you asked me is yes. I would have liked to marry you again."

I heard Dad smirking as I turned my head. "It was great," Dad said. All I could think of was that she was out of my life. Was dad playing some act earlier? I thought to myself.

My Dad cried, and I hugged him again. The video was stopped this time by my father. Man, I have never seen him cry in my whole life. It was almost like a breakdown, so I held on to him tight.

The video started again. "Speaking of good men, that leads me to Oliver," she continued. He sat up straighter and looked expectantly at the screen. "Not to confuse you with a good man, though you are a man," she said with a sniff.

I expected some reaction from him, but Oliver's smirk at me was hardly keeping with the tone in Mother's voice. This wasn't tracking.

"I know you've slept around on me, but at least you were discreet about it," she continued. "Because it's a good idea. I've gone with your advice regarding Sophia." I stiffened in my chair, and Oliver's expression became almost gloating. What advice? I wondered in growing dread.

Mother cut off my internal questions and delivered her pronouncement. "Sophia, some of your behavior Oliver has told me about recently has worried me. I've been afraid you've fallen back in with poor companions. Let me be blunt, dear. I'm afraid you've started retaking drugs." She stared solemnly out of the screen as I gaped in shock. "Oliver convinced me that if you had, I shouldn't support you in destroying yourself, and, for once, I agree with him."

I glared at Oliver. Tony had to pull me back into my seat as I tried to get up to smash his smug face. He'd set me up! Oliver and Daniel had set me up!

Unaware of the unfolding drama in the room, Mother continued to speak. "Your inheritance depends on a clean drug test to be administered here and now. I hate being firm with you, but if you fail this test or refuse to take it, you will inherit one dollar and nothing more."

The lawyer ejected the DVD and put it back in its case. "I have a nurse in the building, and she has a testing kit."

Chapter Twenty-Four

I stood up and glared at Oliver. "Fine, let's get this farce over with." I passed it once this week. This should be no problem. Officer Miller smirked when he looked at Oliver. He knew this was part of the will.

Tony rose to his feet and stopped me, earning a confused look from the lawyer. "I don't trust Oliver. I should take the test first to ensure there's no funny business. Sophia is clean, and so am I.

Surprised, I looked at Oliver. Could he fix this, too?. The lawyer was offended that Tony questioned his integrity. Too bad for him. I sided with Tony, and the lawyer relented. Oliver sat back, still looking very pleased with himself.

Ten minutes later, Tony was back with a woman dressed in scrubs. He just grinned and gave me a thumbs-up as the nurse gave the lawyer the same information in a hushed tone.

"Piece of cake, sweetie," Tony whispered in my ear. "Go in there and settle this once and for all."

I kissed his cheek and nodded. "I'm ready." A female officer was with me when I got to the restroom. And she locked the door behind her.

"Why are you in here?" the nurse asked.

"We both know the answer to that question," the female officer said. This female was six feet and had brown hair and blue eyes. She was pretty and looked like she took great care of herself. Her arms were crossed, and I couldn't see her name tag, but she was someone in charge of what she wanted to do.

Reaching into a box, the nurse pulled out a small plastic cup and handed it to me. "I'm sorry, but I have to see you fill the container," she said apologetically.

That made me smile. I'd probably had more women look at my pussy from far closer than she could guess. "No problem." I quickly filled the cup and handed it over. Then, while she ran her test on my sample, I sat back on the toilet and finished.

The female police officer, with the badge name Smith, took over the test when she found a bottle of what looked like another sample behind the box.

When I emerged from the stall, Officer Smith was cleaning up. She smiled. "All clear, Miss Thomas." Officer Smith was handcuffing the nurse.

"Thank you," I said with a bit of relief. I didn't want to care about getting Mother's money, but part of me still did. Even if the lion's share still went to Oliver, so be it. I guess I couldn't change everything about myself overnight. I followed the officer back to the conference room and glared at Oliver as I sat down. I thought the peacock was going to explode with excitement.

The lawyer nodded to Officer Smith, "I'm taking her down to the station for tampering with someone's drug test." She walked out with a smile directed at me. As soon as the door closed, Mr. Loveless smiled at me.

"Congratulations, Miss Thomas. All clear, as you no doubt expected."

Tony squeezed my hand and said nothing. His smile was worth all this to me.

Oliver leaped to his feet with a screech. "What? Impossible!" He grabbed the table and glared at me. "She fixed the test or paid off the nurse. Call in someone else to do the test. With witnesses!"

The lawyer's smile at Oliver seemed to have a hint of malice under the professional veneer. "I'm very sorry you feel that way, Mister Masterson, but your wife's instructions on this matter are crystal clear. She left the ultimate authority with me. Nurse Granger just informed Officer Smith that changing the test was your idea. You, Masterson, told me it had to be her. I told the police, and they had Sophia watched by two people, not one. The results stand. I will select the appropriate clip to close out Mrs. Masterson's statement if you resume your seat." "The appropriate clip?" Tony asked.

"Indeed," the lawyer replied. "Depending on the outcome of the test, there were two closing videos. I can only play the one dealing with a clean test result. The other will be destroyed by me immediately following the signing of the papers." He slid the second DVD into the player and started the video. My father, who was still there, grabbed my hand and squeezed it like he wanted me to know he was there.

Part of me was still furious with Mother for doubting me, but I had to admit that she probably had good reason. My track record was long and distinguished. I watched her appear and nod at me through the screen.

"I'm sorry I put you through that, Sophia, but I had to be sure." She sounded a little sorry, and I felt my anger toward her melting. "I'm proud of you for staying clean. But it would help if you worked on getting the rest of your life in order. So say 'yes, Mother,'" she said with a smile.

I shook my head at her reproach but said, "Yes, Mother."

"Let's finish this, shall we?" she asked. "Oliver, here is where I deviate from what we discussed." Oliver sat bolt upright. "To my daughter, Sophia, I leave the ranch that I know she loves so much."

Oliver seemed to choke on something, but I barely heard him. My heart was soaring. The ranch meant more to me than I'd been willing to admit. It was a part of me after all these years.

"Seeing as I've already made all the charitable contributions in this life that I care to, that leaves the remainder of my assets, including my home in California that I share with Oliver."

At that, Oliver sat forward. It wasn't delightful, but I would not lose sleep over him getting what he'd schemed over so long. Ultimately, it was more than Dad's fortune since Mother had socked it to him in the divorce, but I had all I wanted. Her love and the ranch would be just fine.

"Those assets," Mother continued blandly, "also go to my daughter, Sophia, except for Oliver's inheritance of one dollar. And don't bother challenging it, Oliver. I have a video of your infidelities, and our prenup is crystal clear on this point."

She sat serenely with her hands folded on her lap as Oliver began shouting and pounding on things. I could only sit there and blink stupidly at the TV. What did she say? I felt like I was having an out-of-body experience - to which I'll admit to some familiarity. From the blinking of Mother's eyes, I knew the video wasn't paused, so she was waiting for the scene to calm.

Oliver stormed out of the conference room with shouted threats of lawsuits and appeals and left us at relative peace. Mother sat quietly for another half-minute before continuing.

"Well, I'm betting Oliver has left. No doubt in quite a temper," she said dryly. "He never was as smart as he thought he was. Sophia..." I swallowed and waited. "The last thing I'll leave you is a piece of advice. Could you not make the same mistake I did? Don't mistake existence for life. Find someone you can love. Forget what anyone expects of you. To hell with them. Find someone you love and stay with them," she grimaced in distaste, "even if it is a woman."

I laughed and hugged Tony to me. If only she were here! As sad as it was, her passing made me see exactly what she was telling me.

"I love you." She smiled affectionately, and the screen went dark.

The lawyer rose, pulled out the DVD, and handed me the ones we'd viewed. "The unviewed disc will be destroyed after you sign next to the arrows on these papers." He also took one of the two papers from the folder before calling in his secretary to witness. I suppose those papers would've given Oliver his heart's desire.

Tony stood and put his hands on my shoulders while I signed the documents. It was odd how you could throw your life away and find it anew.

The lawyer handed the unneeded DVD and papers to his secretary to destroy. "If you'll excuse me for a moment?" At my nod, he followed her out, quietly closing the door behind him.

"I could never have made it through this without you," I told Tony. "And I'd have slipped and given Oliver everything he wanted if you hadn't been there."

He kissed my neck. "All I did was help you help yourself. It was your strength that beat him. That beat both of them."

"Officer Miller, can my dad read that before you take it with you?" I asked.

"I don't see why not," Officer Miller said.

"Sophia, I would like to stay with you for a while and help you in any way I can," Dad said.

"I would like that," I said and hugged my dad. That made me feel even better. "What letter?" Officer Miller took dad aside, gave the letter, and explained that he needed to read it, and dad sat in the chair and started reading. I knew when he was done when he was swearing and ready to kill someone. For the first time in my life, my father truly loved my mom, so I will give him a chance to make it right.

When the lawyer returned, we shook hands. I asked him to lock the bank accounts and secure all of Mother's—my properties from Oliver, both physically and legally. After that, Tony, my Dad, and I will take care of evicting Oliver from the ranch and taking Daniel out too. "Mister Thomas, there is one thing left for you. It was brought in two days before your wife's death, and I am told to give it to you. Can you sign this paper, and the letter is all yours."

Chapter Twenty-Five

Sitting in Tony's Rover after we left the lawyer's office, I tried to get my bearings. Although the past hour's events were still too overwhelming for me, I wondered what was on the disk?

I need to focus on the here and now. Perhaps I'll work up the courage and talk to Miller tomorrow about seeing the disk and learning what's on it. But, first, we'd best go to the ranch and see to throwing out the trash. Then, see about calling a locksmith. That last one was a good thought, and I didn't want to wait. Grabbing my cell, I called the locksmith, and he said he be there in an hour. I was being charged a time and a half, but that's an extra charge I could live with.

"Let's deal with our unwanted house guests," I told Tony. His answering grin was almost shark-like, and he drove there quickly.

The driveway had Daniel's rental and Oliver's SUV in it. I wondered briefly where he'd found it. Officer Miller asked my Dad to go to the station and talk to him about several things.

He said he was coming back after.

I climbed out with a shrug. No matter. It would be a pleasure to throw Daniel out, too. I went through the front door and heard Oliver shouting in the great room. They must be arguing.

Perfect. I went up the stairs quietly, with Tony beside me.

Daniel was standing in the center of the room, his arms folded, staring coldly at Oliver. Oliver was pouring himself a drink and hurling abuses at Daniel.

"If you call me incompetent one more time," Daniel snarled, cutting Oliver off mid-curse, "I'll stuff that damned bottle up your ass. It's not my fault she didn't use the coke."

"But you swore she did," Oliver protested, his back still to all of us. This was exciting stuff, indeed.

"I said she seemed to have taken it," Daniel sneered. "That you're idiot enough to count on assumptions isn't my problem. I'm only here to give her payback for dumping me. Likewise, I don't believe that you couldn't hide the fact you killed your wife is my fault at all, too. What happens to you is your problem."

"Shut up, dumb ass," Oliver began. "They would have never found out if it hadn't been for that dumb-ass tech taking the bad blood. The bitch was going back to her ex-husband, leaving me nothing. You're in this too as much as I am, and you know it."

"Phoebe would not have died if Karla hadn't given her that lethal dosage," Daniel said.

"What the hell!" I said in my head. Then I thought like my mother would and pulled out my cell and looked to see if the videos in the house were still on, and they were. I took the last ten minutes of the video and sent it to my father because he was at the police station. Then I made one that had thirty minutes and sent it to my dad. I didn't have Officer Miller's phone number on my cell, but I thought dad would see it and do something. I heard a vase crash that had been thrown across the room. Then I heard more yelling, and I had enough.

"You gentlemen," I said in a clear, firm voice that yanked both of their eyes to me, "and I use that term very loosely, are on private property." Oliver dropped the bottle, and it shattered loudly in the sudden silence.

While Oliver looked like a mouse staring at a snake, frozen in fear, Daniel smiled. He always used the same smile when he'd gotten away with something.

He sauntered over to stand in front of me. The arrogance of his stance stood my teeth on edge, but I didn't want to argue. I just wanted him gone.

"Looks like you came up roses again, babe."

"Get your things and get out, Daniel," I said frostily. "Now."

His grin raised my hackles. "What you want is no skin off my nose. You should know by now that I don't do what you tell me. "

"I know if you did, you would be better in bed, and I can say you suck at sex," I said.

As the rage toward Daniel flared up inside me, I had even less warning than Daniel when Tony's arm shot past me, and a hard-knuckled fist exploded against Daniel's nose. I swear I could see it flatten and twist slowly as blood squirted. Daniel flew back and crashed into a coffee table on his way to the floor. That had to hurt. Daniel struggled to get his feet under him and shot a murderous glare at Tony.

I wanted to kick him while he was down, but he was back on his feet too quickly.

"I suppose you think I deserved that," he sneered at me. "Fine, you keep on believing that."

Tony advanced on Daniel, his expression promising pain. Daniel backed up, holding up one hand. "This is Oliver's problem, not mine. I'm leaving because my business here is done."

Part of me was very disappointed. I wanted to see Daniel pay, but people like him never did. At least I was through with him once and for all. Good riddance. Tony followed him out while I glared at Oliver.

"You were poisoning my mom and killed her."

"I didn't kill her. I just helped her cancer along," Oliver said.

"You can leave under your power right now, and I ship your crap to you, or we toss you out, too," I said serenely. "Please make me throw you out. Pretty please?"

"You'll have that muscle-bound oaf hit me?" he sniffed. "This isn't over by any means. I've already called my attorney to get the will overturned. You may have..."

Even as I stepped up to him, I wasn't sure what I was doing. The impact of my knee on his crotch was almost as much a surprise to me as it was to him.

Oliver's eyes bulged, and he collapsed in a heap, groaning and writhing.

"You are one of three that killed my mom; you're going to prison," I said.

"There is no proof," Oliver said, and I kicked him in the stomach. I stepped back, stunned at my actions. I didn't get into fights. That was so not me. I firmly suppressed the satisfaction I was feeling.

Tony walked back up the stairs, dusting his hand off in a symbolic gesture. "That's it for him. He took off like..." He stopped, staring at us. I tried not to look smug. "I see you and Oliver have finished your little talk." He grinned at me with an expression that just oozed approval. "Let's see him out."

Tony grabbed Oliver by the collar and pulled him to his feet. I followed them as he frog-marched the unresisting Oliver to the driveway. Then he stuffed him into that crappy white SUV of his. I suppose I could've made him walk and kept the car, but it hardly seemed worth the trouble.

Oliver was coordinated enough to get it started and drive away when five police cars showed up and stopped Oliver, and took him away.

I turned to Tony and pulled him into my arms. "I can't imagine karma bringing you into my life, so it must be redeemed."

He smiled at me. "It is our redemption and their bad karma returning to roost."

We'd melted together and had only begun kissing when my cell phone rang. I groaned theatrically and pulled it off my belt. "Sophia."

"Oh, my God," Emma said into my ear. "Sophia, I'm so sorry! I just heard the news! I'll be on a plane as soon as I can. Are you okay? Where do you want me to meet you?"

I smiled at Tony while he held me. "Emma, calm down and take a breath. It's okay. I'm doing fine. Don't cut your trip short. Come see me when you return, and we'll talk then." I kissed Tony on the lips softly. "I have the most amazing thing to tell you, but it can wait. So then, I will see you. Call me." Then I hung up before my stunned friend could ask me questions I wasn't ready to answer.

Tony whispered in my ear. "You love Emma?"

I looked into Tony's eyes with a smile. "Yes, I love her. I love Charlotte, too. I can't wait for you to meet them." Exploring the similarities and differences of loving a man would be interesting. I couldn't wait for them to meet Tony.

"The locksmith should be here soon, and we need to arrange for a maid, maybe an assistant for Ms. Johnson, for the ranch. I know of a young soon-to-be mother that would be perfect for the job."

Tony kissed me thoroughly and led me back into the house. As we left the door open for my father, approaching, followed by Officer Miller followed us in. "You better tell me your intentions for my daughter," Dad said. I smirked, then the sound of the door closing behind us reminded me that when one door closed, another opened to my new life.

About the Author

Tammy Godfrey has called Southeast Idaho home for the vast majority of her life. She survived sixteen years in the military, and she is proud of almost every minute of it. After leaving the camouflage uniform behind she decided she needed to do something productive with the time tat she wasn't taking care of her husband and kids. When she wasn't lost in the exciting world of tax preparation, she was hitting the books at Idaho State University seeking a degree in something practical like business. During her time in the world of academia she discovered a love for writing. After spending long days and nights overcoming her fear of the blank page her first book was published in 2013. She is currently working hard on her next novel. Tammy loves everything geek, including her adorable husband, and loves working on crafty things, reading, and going to comic con. Tammy believes that Murphy's Law has played a large part in her life. If anything weird can happen, it will. One thing that can be said about Tammy Godfrey, she's not boring.

Also by Tammy Godfrey

Finding A Geek For My Very Own

Tiara loved going to comic book conventions every year, however this year Tiara's best friend Carrie is changing things up by making her go to speed dating. Yes, I know speed dating, Tiara wanted to throw-up. She wasn't asking for a hot guy, they're too much trouble. Tiara wants a guy that's into D&D,

conventions, cosplay, SciFi movies, binge-worthy TV shows, and comic books, vintage and new. In other words, a geek. There are three times the amount of nerd guys than nerd girls, and still she couldn't hook one. But things change. Her eyes catch a gleam from the cosplay armor of Iron Man, and meets Adam, the man behind the mask. His power: the ability to make her heartbeat like a jack hammer. Has she found a geek for her very own? Adam comes to the comic book convention every year with his friends and family. After he beholds a beautiful Mother of Dragons, his purpose is clear - talk to her. Most women that come to these events have boyfriends, but this one was on her own. Adam realizes that the woman of his fantasy is real when she passes the ultimate test. She meets the family and survives the judgment of friends. But with the light of newfound love comes the dark. She is Dakota, aka The Ex. She was paid to be a cosplay girl, but her real agenda was clear. Get Adam back or dash the hopes for anyone else.

Milton Keynes UK
Ingram Content Group UK Ltd.
UKHW041318061224
3480UKWH00024B/43